Miranda Jones thought she was on track.

Her career as an artist had gotten off to a slow start and now is finally beginning to gather momentum. Featured in a good San Francisco gallery, and signed with a reputable artist's representative, her prospects for earning look bright and her reputation is growing as a painter of both landscapes and wildlife.

But something still feels off kilter. The subjects of her work all live in nature, yet she herself lives in the city. Her rep and her family emphasize money as the benchmark of success, yet her own goals have to do with the professional challenges of excellence, adventure, and authenticity.

Miranda and Meredith are as different as night and day.

Yet their helpful mother arranges for them to become roommates. Where Meredith speeds through life super-charged with energy and ambition, Miranda moves with slow deliberation, stepping with utmost care through the details of her art. Though they share a familial history of privilege, Meredith embraces her status, leveraging every opportunity, while Miranda side-steps any possibility of personal gain unless it's hard won and benefits others as well.

Milford-Haven shimmers afar as an unfulfilled dream.

It lurks in the heart of the artist, an unformed possibility. Not even Miranda herself knows what lies shrouded in a misty future, with a legacy stretching back to ancestral roots and untapped cellular memory.

When forces larger than any she could have imagined begin to exert a pull powerful enough to bring ancient desires to the surface, Miranda paints a simple watercolor and pins it to the wall of her studio.

Why is the little picture so important? What will happen when this imaginary image draws her inexorably to its shores? What changes might this spark in her life?

Come discover what happens . . . ***When the Heart Listens.***

THE PRESS PRAISES MARA PURL'S
MILFORD-HAVEN NOVELS & NOVELLAS

"Former *Days of Our Lives* star Purl presents the first novel in her Milford-Haven series, which . . . features a setting of unadulterated beauty—the small coastal town of Milford-Haven, CA in the prosperous mid-'90s—and a cast of successful, sexy, sometimes quirkily independent characters. . . . Readers will find details galore . . . and the novel's many inner monologues reveal scheming, secretly confused, or flawed personalities. . . . Milford-Haven offers depictions of daily life, hints of possible future romance, the threat of scandal, and carefully parsed out mystery. . . . The novel is poised to convince readers to continue with the series."
– Publishers Weekly

"Former *Days of Our Lives* actress Purl imbues her soap opera finesse into the fictional setting of Milford-Haven, a sleepy California coastal town. This may be Apple Pie, USA, but hearts are on the line, professions are at stake and a possible murder has tainted the landscape. A whirlwind of juicy drama with dangling-carrot closure." *– Kirkus Review*

"*What the Heart Knows* is an upbeat novel . . . the first book of Milford-Haven. The book opens powerfully . . . Purl does not use external paraphernalia to bring her characters to life. Multiple love stories, friendships, crushes. . . . Purl's characters are well-traveled, educated, and street smart."
– ForeWord Magazine

". . . in Mara Purl's enchanting novel *What the Heart Knows* . . . although the picturesque, seaside setting of Milford-Haven plays an important role in the novel, the cast of interesting and eccentric characters is what really draws the reader into the book." *– Bookwire*

"Mara Purl's *What the Heart Knows* is a first class novel by a very talented writer with strong believable characters, a rapid-pace delivery of story, and very tight writing that make this novel such a delight to read. . . . I look forward to seeing other titles in this impressive series."
– Gary Roen, Nationally Syndicated Book Reviewer

"In *Where the Heart Lives,* Mara Purl strategically presents a glamorous alternative to big city vibrancy. In the second installment of her already popular Milford-Haven series, the California Central Coast is once again the locale for her magnetic cast of characters. Purl's success is based on her ability to appeal to readers on a more elevated level than traditional romance fiction generally prescribes. Though she never loses the common touch in her storytelling instincts, in every potential stereotype emerges a well-developed character with a standout personality."   *– ForeWord Reviews*

"[In] the second volume of this ongoing saga . . . Purl returns to picturesque Milford-Haven. The town is filled with back stories—dark secrets, hidden agendas, failed romances and budding love, not to mention the unsolved mystery. Skillfully interspersing the moment-to-moment thoughts of her characters with their actions and dialogue, Purl effortlessly moves from one personal story to another. Like visiting friends and catching up. . . ."   *– Kirkus Review*

"Part small-town confidential, part mystery, part romance, the story is cozy in the best sense of the word. Steeped in California charm, the setting plays host to a wide variety of characters from across the social spectrum. High society rubs shoulders with artists and diner cooks, providing a snap shot of an up-scale village. Despite the town's air of quaint charm, the people are refreshingly realistic."   *– Bookwire*

"[In] the second Milford-Haven novel, award-winning writer Mara Purl deepens the intrigue in this captivating window into the little battles, victories, successes, and failings of ordinary people in [the] complicated world [of] Milford-Haven."
– Midwest Book Review

"Once again Purl pulls out all the stops and goes straight to the heart of the story. This is the where it all began—Miranda's quest for the life she wasn't aware she wanted and needed. The descriptions are so spot on you can almost feel you are in the flower fields in Central California, I could taste the food at French Laundry, and could picture the murals in Miranda's space in the house she shares with her sister. Sibling relationships are complicated at best, and Purl offers the perfect mix of closeness and rivalry. It's also very comforting to know that listening to your heart over your common sense is, at times, the right thing to do."
– Linda Thompson, Host of TheAuthorsShow.com

The *Milford-Haven Novel* Series

"In Mara Purl's books the writing is crisp and clean, the dialogue realistic, the scenes well described. I salute her ingenuity." **– Bob Johnson, Former Managing Editor The Associated Press**

"Every reader who enjoys book series about small town life has a treat to anticipate in . . . Mara Purl's *Milford-Haven Novels*." **– Dee Ann Ray, *The Clinton Daily News***

"Mara Purl's characters have become old friends and I keep expecting one of them to give me a call!" **– Nanci Cone, *Ventura Breeze***

". . . an intrigu[ing] cast of diverse characters." **– Fred Klein, *Santa Barbara News Press***

"You can't escape the pull of Milford-Haven, the setting for *Days of Our Lives* actress and award-winning author Mara Purl's enticing new novel *What the Heart Knows*. My kind of romance, this [is a] juicy read . . . plus, the inviting story makes you *think*." **– Charlotte Hill, *Boomer Brief***

"I read Mara Purl's *What the Heart Knows* and loved the book—just devoured it, in fact—and can't wait to read the next installment." **– Anne L. Holmes, APR National Association of Baby Boomer Women**

ENDORSEMENTS FROM OTHER AUTHORS

"Mara Purl is a skillful storyteller who has written a charming and tantalizing saga about the ways in which lives can intersect and be forever changed. The first novel in the saga is not-to-be-missed." **– Margaret Coel *New York Times* best-selling author of the *Wind River Mysteries***

"I found a kinship with . . . your heart for character . . . and with your truly fine unveiling of story events." **– Jane Kirkpatrick, Author Wrangler Award, Willa Award**

"I so admire Mara Purl's writing style. The pictures she paints are just glorious, her characters and attention to detail inspiring." **– Sheri Anderson Emmy Award-winning writer, *Days of Our Lives* Author, *Salem Secrets Series***

COMMENTS FROM READERS OF
WHEN THE HEART LISTENS

"This might be the most awesome book in the Milford-Haven series so far. While reading, I was envying artist-protagonist Miranda's discovery of finding her sense of place. And reading the plein air painting chapter gave me little chilblains down my arms and made my painting fingers twitch. Nice job!"

– Mary Helsaple
Watermedia IX Silver Medal Award, Washington Ad Press
Silver Award for World Wildlife brochure, Winner –
Gateway to Sedona Artist Competition, artist for Grand Canyon
Land Trust, Artists in Normandy, & Milford-Haven Novels

COMMENTS FROM LISTENERS OF
WHAT THE HEART KNOWS
THE AUDIO BOOK
Winner – Silver – Benjamin Franklin Award – Adult
Fiction/Audio

"Your audio book of *What the Heart Knows* is a thoroughly satisfying and engrossing listen! Your marvelous vocal character delineations (I loved the gravelly 'Jack' and the quirky Southern 'Sally')—and your plot twists and turns—kept me 'all ears' for many hours of entertainment!"

– Stephanie Zimbalist, Actress, Los Angeles

"I just loved, *loved* your book on tape. I am a real fan of yours now. One gets so drawn into the stories and the characters that you've created. I couldn't wait to get into the car and to listen to it."

– Linda Meadows, Artist, Los Angeles

ACCOLADES FOR *MILFORD-HAVEN, U.S.A.*
the hit BBC radio series

"Mara Purl's mix of a soap-opera format . . . is a smash hit in Britain."

– The Los Angeles Times

"A sudsy look at today's toughest issues."

– The Hollywood Reporter

"A slice of life in 'small-town U.S.A.' includes well-known cast members and music artists like the Doobie Brothers."

– Billboard

When the
Heart Listens

Also by MARA PURL

Fiction

Milford-Haven Novels
What the Heart Knows (Book One)
Where the Heart Lives (Book Two)
Why Hearts Keep Secrets (Book Three)

Milford-Haven Novellas & Novelettes
When the Heart Listens
When Hummers Dream
When Whales Watch
When Otters Play

Milford-Haven Paranormal Novellas
What the Soul Suspects
Where the Soul Journeys

Milford-Haven Holiday Novellas & Novelettes
When Angels Paint
Where an Angel's on a Rope
Whose Angel Key Ring
Christmas Angels
A Milford-Haven Story Collection
The Milford-Haven Novels: Early Editions

Non-Fiction

Act Right: A Manual for the On-Camera Actor
(with Erin Gray)

Kenneth Leventhal & Co.: A History of the Firm

S.T.A.R.—Student Theatre & Radio
High School Curriculum; College Curriculum

Plays	Screenplays & Teleplays	Radio Plays
Mary Shelley—	*The Meridian Factor*	*Milford-Haven, U.S.A.*
In Her Own Words	(with Verne Nobles)	(100 episodes)
(with Sydney Swire)	*Welcome to Milford-Haven*	*Green Valley*
Dracula's Last Tour	(with Katherine	*Haven Ten*
	Doughtie Nolan)	**S.T.A.R.**
		Teleplay
	Guiding Light	*Only A Test*

S.T.A.R. Radio Plays

America the Beautiful   *In or Out*
Ashton Valley   *The Journal*
Boom   *K-RAP*
Caught in a Web   *Love Child*
Changes   *Love Resolutions*
Cruising   *The New Girl*
The Curse of Santa Florida   *The Peak Mystery*
Deep Freeze   *San Feliz*
Fountain Hills Mall   *Secretos*
Friendz   *Tokyo Time Travel*
Frozen Hearts   *Toxicity*
The Game   *Westland High*
Going Somewhere   *Wrong Way*

Mara Purl

When the Heart Listens

A Milford-Haven Novella

Bellekeep Books

When the Heart Listens ©2009 & 2019 by Mara Purl

Milford-Haven PUBLISHING, RECORDING & BROADCASTING HISTORY
This book is based upon the original radio drama Milford-Haven *©1987 by Mara Purl, Library of Congress numbers SR188828, SR190790, SR194010; and upon the original radio drama* Milford-Haven, U.S.A. *©1992 by Mara Purl, Library of Congress number SR232-483, broadcast by the British Broadcasting Company's BBC Radio 5 Network, and which is also currently in release in audio formats as* Milford-Haven, U.S.A. *©1992 by Mara Purl. Portions of this material may also appear on the Milford-Haven Web Site, www.MilfordHaven.com, or on www.MaraPurl.com © by Mara Purl.*
All rights reserved.
Portions of this work were published in early editions.
Test-Marketing Novelization Edition Copyright © 1997 by Mara Purl
Library of Congress Txu-766-374
Early Edition Copyright © 2005 by Mara Purl
Library of Congress TX 6-452-073

Names: Purl, Mara, author.
Title: When the heart listens / Mara Purl.
Other Titles: Milford-Haven U.S.A. (Radio program) | Milford-Haven (Radio program)
Description: New York, NY : Bellekeep Books, [2019] | Series: A Milford-Haven novella | Based upon the original radio dramas Milford-Haven and Milford-Haven U.S.A., broadcast by BBC Radio 5 Network. | Prequel to: Milford-Haven novels.
Identifiers: ISBN 9781936878802
Subjects: LCSH: Women painters--California--Fiction. | City and town life--California--Fiction. | Interpersonal relations--Fiction. | Intuition--Fiction. | California--Fiction.
Classification: LCC PS3566.U75 W441 2019 | DDC 813/.6--dc23

Published in print edition in the U.S. by Bellekeep Books, New York
www.BellekeepBooks.com
Published in audio in the U.S. by Haven Books, Los Angeles   www.HavenBooks.net
10 9 8 7 6 5 4 3 2
Printed in the United States of America

This book is dedicated to the well-read and savvy women who belong to book clubs. Special thanks for your thoughtful reading of my books, and gracious invitations for speaking. Your listening showed me I had to write this story.

Acknowledgments

Thanks to my publishers: Patrice Samara, Kara Johnson, and Tara Goff at Bellekeep for vision, guidance and faith. Thanks to my gifted editorial team: Vicki Hessel Werkley, Jean Laidig and Laurie Jameson, and to Jean again for interior design. Thanks to Mary Helsaple for exquisite watercolors for my book covers, to Reya Patton and Kevin Meyer for designing the original cover templates, and to Nick Zelinger for taking over to create beautiful covers. Thanks to my marketing team: Jonatha King at King Communications for PR and marketing; Kelly Johnson for Internet and social media wizardry; Sky Esser and Amber Ludwig for web design. Thanks to Kathy Meis at Bublish for marketing wisdom. And thanks to friend, colleague, and mentor Judith Briles for leadership and support.

Thanks to those who provide expertise during my research: for "Miranda," to artists Mary Helsaple and Caren Pearson, and to Dennis Curry and Rosanne Seitz of S.L.O.P.E. (San Luis Obispo Painters for the Environment) for inspiration and depth of detail; to Dennis Eamon Young and Carol Schmidt for the Carrizo Plain National Monument research trip; and to Vickie Zoellner for financial industry backround.

San Francisco, though never my home city, has always been a favorite destination. Thanks to Victoria Zackheim, noted writer and editor, for hosting me during several wonderful recent visits; to the late Jane Rees, dear family friend and *Japan Times* columnist through decades in Tokyo and the City By the Bay; and family friend Maureen D'Honau for her San Francisco real estate wisdom. The 1995 setting of this novella necessitated research into the fascinating, booming mid-1990s. Craig Newmark did indeed found his CraigsList in 1995, but my character's working for him is fictional. The French Laundry Restaurant was the 1994 choice on Michael Bauer's list "30 Most Important Bay Area Restaurants of the Last 30 Years." I did not refer to the glorious book *The French Laundry*, because it wasn't published until 1999. I did enjoy the Anthony Bourdain video of the legendary visit he and other accomplished chefs paid as guests of Chef Thomas Keller. My gifted friend John Rhys-Davies did portray Leonardo da Vinci in *Star Trek: Voyager*, but not until 1997, so I apologize for taking poetic license in placing the broadcast two years early. The artist Gerard D'A. Henderson is represented truthfully in this book, as both renowned artist and long-time family friend. A wonderful website chronicling his extraordinary career is kept up to date. What a privilege it was to share his exuberance and friendship.

Thanks to dear friends in the Central Coast who've supported Milford-Haven for many years with such enthusiasm, including Elaine Travel Evans, Kathe Tanner, Susan Berry, Judy Salamacha,

Dennis Eamon Young, and Carol Schmidt; to my colleagues at Central Coast Sisters in Crime, and at SLO Night Writers.

Thanks to Verne Nobles, and to Frank Abatemarco for clear vision and passionate commitment to the Milford-Haven Television project.

Thanks to sponsors and co-hosts past and future for helping me produce the Milford-Haven Chari-Tea® Events (Possibili-Teas, Generosi-Teas, Hospitali-Teas, Creativi-Teas, Connective-Teas, and our list continues!)

And most important of all—thanks to *you*, my readers! I'm thrilled to welcome those of you who are new to my books. I continue to learn from you, and to appreciate your steadfast support during my publishing journey.

The Radio Drama

The Milford-Haven Podcast, now at long last makes its debut so American listeners can hear the show. *Milford-Haven* began as a radio drama with an initial air date in 1987 on KOTR in Cambria, California, our first radio home. In its next incarnation, *Milford-Haven, U.S.A.* leapt "the pond" and was broadcast on the BBC as the first American serial available for UK audiences. My thanks to Ms. Pat Ewing, Director of Radio 5—a maverick network that launched a maverick show and celebrated with us when we reached 4.5 million listeners.

In the U.S., thanks to New York's Museum of TV & Radio and Chicago's Museum of Broadcast Communications, for honoring the show by adding it to their permanent collections. The show enjoyed revivals at YesterdayUSA.com, KTEA in Cambria, and Air America's premiere Inland Empire station.

I'm thrilled to announce that, at long last, the show is available via podcast! I invite you to visit www.MilfordHaven.com, where you may browse or start your subscription.

Before there were any shows to air, there were talented actors, and my thanks go to both the original cast of *Milford-Haven* and to the cast of *Milford-Haven, U.S.A.*, seasoned professionals who brought my characters so vividly to life that their work is inextricably woven into the fabric of the characters themselves.

Before there were actors to record, there had to be a studio, and my thanks to Engineer Bill Berkuta, whose Afterhours Recording Company became our studio home—a workshop in which we created one hundred episodes of the first show, sixty of the second, fifty Student Theater & Radio (S.T.A.R.) productions, and now scores of audio books, audio dramas, and podcasts.

Thanks to Marilyn Harris and Mark Wolfram, who composed the haunting *Milford-Haven* theme and all the music cues that supported the emotional ebb and flow of the story, and whose music we now use for the *Milford-Haven Novels* Audio Books.

And before there was a *Milford-Haven*, there was a young woman who had always lived in cities—Tokyo, New York, Los Angeles. I spent a summer performing *Sea Marks* at Jim and Olga Buckley's Pewter Plough Playhouse in Cambria, and became fascinated with life in and of a small town.

Thanks to my U.S. listeners, especially those in Cambria and the Central Coast. Thanks to my U.K. listeners, particularly those in Milford Haven, Wales. Both these special towns have embraced me as an honorary citizen.

Thanks to my family and friends—supportive from day one: my late parents Ray & Marshie Purl, Linda Purl, Erin Gray, Caren Pearson, with very special thanks to Miranda Kenrick, and to Vickie Zoellner. My love and thanks to my husband Larry Norfleet.

And finally, thanks to my characters, among whom are: Jack, Zack, Miranda, Zelda, Samantha, Sally, Kevin, Joseph, Cornelius, Meredith, Shelley, June, Chris, Burt, Delmar, Emily, Wilhelm, Stacey, James, Mary, Russell, Nicole, Susan, and Cynthia . . . who are building, buying, painting, conniving, planning, dishing, cogitating, dominating, observing, consulting, beach-combing, serving, sleuthing, skulking, detecting, reporting, abusing, enduring, nurturing, scheduling, ordering, showing, sneaking and seducing, respectively.

Dear Reader —

Welcome to Milford-Haven! Whether you're a first-time or returning visitor, it is my pleasure to introduce you to my favorite little town as my protagonist arrives there, so you can see it with eyes as fresh as hers. You'll meet some of the people in her life, many of whom are described in the Cast of Characters for the series near the end of the book.

This novella features artist Miranda Jones, and the life she's leading in San Francisco just before moving to what will become her new home in a small, sparkling jewel of a coastal town. The story stands alone as a complete tale, but is woven into the overall tapestry of the Milford-Haven saga. Chronologically, *When the Heart Listens* takes place just before *When Hummers Dream*, and before the first novel of the saga, *What the Heart Knows*. You'll find preview chapters waiting for you at the end of this short book.

As this story reveals, Miranda is an artist who focuses on the outdoors and her canvases feature the wildlife creatures she loves to study and observe. During her frequent forays into nature, she captures images on film that later come to life in her studio as animal portraits and as landscapes.

But her city life, at odds with her nature-focus, still is helping her to create a unique ability to paint not only landscapes, but mindscapes. In this tale, she paints views that should be there, but aren't until she creates them. Is it this unique talent that leads her to a most unusual experience—that of precognitive painting? She paints an "inscape," defined as the unique essence or inner nature of a place depicted in a work of art. Little does she know that the *inscape* she sees in her mind's eye is something she'll later see physically manifested as a familiar landscape.

In future novels and stories, we'll travel with Miranda into the flow of a young woman looking to create the life she truly wants, revealing what she'll have to do to build her dream.

As this novella unfolds, follow my footsteps over the interconnected pathways of those who inhabit Milford-Haven, and come to that place where transformation can bring about the very goals we've been desiring . . . when we let our hearts listen.

Mara Purl

Part I
1994

"Listen to your heart, for it knows the way."
– *Jennifer Williamson*

Chapter 1

Veronica Jones lifted the monogrammed napkin from her lap and touched it to the corners of her mouth. Folding the smooth cloth in half, she pulled it through the silver napkin ring that bore the same initials as the linen.

Veri, as her family and friends called her, looked across the small table at her husband of many years—still handsome and straight-backed, the gray at his temples lending a distinguished touch to his sculpted face.

"I've got to do something about the girls," she said, eyeing the coffee pot and considering whether she'd allow herself another half cup.

"You're always doing something about the girls," Charles said, not even looking over the top of the *San Francisco Chronicle* he read religiously every morning.

"You know what I mean, Charles. One is living in that icy tower of glass; the other is practically buried in that basement. Neither of them is truly happy. Neither is really safe."

Charles folded his paper and looked into her eyes.

"Don't fret, dear. They're grown women, now. You can't live their lives for them. You can't tell them what to do."

From his mollifying tone, and from the softness of his expression, she knew he sympathized. Still, his words rankled. She couldn't bear the idea of not being able to help her daughters—whether or not they asked. She had, in fact, come up with a plan. Well, a partial plan. Though she had no intention of revealing details to their father just yet, she did think a mention might be politic.

"Uh-oh," he said, shaking his head while he poured himelf a fresh cup of coffee. "You're up to something. Let's have it."

"Well," she began, "it would save them both money, and they'd be far more secure."

Veri smiled, and when her husband squinted, she saw with satisfaction that amusement was already beginning to coax a smile at the edges of his mouth.

Good. I'll make him my co-conspirator before he even knows what he's sanctioning.

Meredith Jones pressed the button for 22 and closed her eyes as a gust of wind swirled through the lobby and sent a blast into the elevator. April breezes howled through the shaft until the doors fully closed, and she felt her heart lurch right along with the car as it climbed through the lower floors.

With a "ding," the doors flew open and she stepped onto the faux-marble floor, then clacked down the hallway to her unit, wrinkling her nose at the cooking smells that clung to the wallpaper in the corridor. Sliding the key into her lock, she pushed open her door and flung off her high heels even before the metal front door slammed shut behind her.

"Ahh," she said aloud, dropping her briefcase, throwing her coat over the back of a bar stool, and opening the fridge. She reached inside for a half-finished bottle of Chardonnay, poured herself a glass, then settled on the sofa, wiggling her toes as she stretched her legs across the cushions.

Missed it again, she thought, bemoaning that she never managed to get home in time to see the sunset. *But what little I saw from the car was gorgeous.*

For a new VP of client relations at a high-powered financial management firm, working late came with the territory. Still, she felt entitled to complain in the privacy of her own apartment. When her stomach rumbled, she remembered that bellyaching wouldn't put food on her table.

"Pizza Palace?" she wondered aloud. They did have a great Italian salad. Szechuan Sensations sounded more appealing, though, and she stepped to the kitchen counter, picked up the handset with her favorite restaurants programmed into the speed-dial function, and placed the call.

By the time she'd changed into her dove-gray sweat pants and zippered top, prepared a tray, and turned on her TV, the intercom began buzzing.

A few minutes later, while she deftly picked at her Szechuan chicken and spicy string beans, she rewound the tape in her VCR and hit play, laughing out loud when Kramer, looking as if he'd just stuck his finger in an electrical outlet, walked across the hall and into Jerry's apartment to ask an inane question. It was a show about . . . nothing, Meredith decided, which was why she enjoyed watching it. How else could she take her mind off the daily stress and unwind?

Suddenly the crisp bite of spicy chicken trapped between her chop sticks didn't look as delicious as it had a moment earlier. *I've managed to avoid thinking about it for a whole hour and half, and now it's back, dammit.*

Albert Rothman, recently named senior partner—and the youngest ever to be so named—knew how brilliant he was, how valuable to the firm, and he had his eye on wealth to rival sultans. But he had a blind spot about his sex appeal. Convinced any woman would be grateful to be blessed by his attentions, he'd so far managed only to offend "lesser" employees, each of whom had been quietly dismissed with an attractive financial bonus. And Meredith only knew about these arrangements because she herself had now made partner.

Today, however, he'd managed to offend her twice, in two distinct ways. First, he'd questioned her data interpretation at her debut partner presentation. Though it'd stung, she'd accepted the criticism graciously, acknowledging the new alpha dog, flattering him by treating him as leader, though in truth he was only a couple of years older than she.

Second, he'd propositioned her. *Talk about a no-win scenario*, Meredith thought bitterly. She knew perfectly well how the game was played: be charming, but not overtly flirtatious; dress in a way that was appealing but not sexy; do your work better than any of the male partners.

A mentor had once said to her, "Meredith, in this business you have to be either very good, or very bad." She hadn't understood what he meant at first, so he'd explained. "If you plan to sleep your way to the top, be strategic and don't get emotionally involved. If you *don't* plan to use sex to get ahead, be sure not to sleep with *anyone* to get ahead. It'll be used against you."

Best advice I ever got, she mused. She'd adhered to his suggestion, and never dated anyone at the firm. In fact, she felt professional behavior at work was the gold standard. She also felt that what she did on her own time was her own business.

She glanced at her chopsticks as though she had no idea what to do with them and set them aside as her thoughts came back to Albert. Their paths were entwined at work. Would she be interested in dating him if not? Her instincts told her he was too self-involved and thought too little of women to truly hold her interest. In any case, because of their work connection, the point was moot. Her own personal rules wouldn't allow involvement with him.

So where did that leave her now? *Damned if I do, damned if I don't.* If she turned him down, he'd take offence, and try his best to take it out of her career performance, one way or another. If she accepted his invitation—drink and dinner for now, but who knows what he really expected—she'd be stepping into a quagmire.

"Hell with it," she said, pressing the fast forward button on her remote. "I'm not going out with that man."

She took a deep breath and looked out the picture window at the view of the city now sparkling against a field of black. Between adjacent tall buildings, she could see the string of lights outlining the Golden Gate Bridge.

If she lost her job, she'd certainly have to move out of this apartment with its privileged views. But that wouldn't be the end of the world.

With the mental toughness that'd ensured her rapid ascent in a male-dominated career, she refused to think about Albert any longer. Instead, she swept away the debris of her dinner, took a hot bath, set her alarm, and curled up with a steamy romance novel. In her fantasies, a real relationship with a good man was well within the realm of possibility.

Miranda Jones pushed more Cadmium Yellow Medium Hue paint from the tube onto her palette. To it, she added a touch of Hansa Yellow, then experimented by using her brush to swipe through a touch of Naples, just to see whether the mixture would give her the variation of depth she wanted.

She loved the Daniel Smith paint: how luminous and

vividly transparent they were, how easy to work with, and how permanent the hues. She also liked that she could get the same array of colors, whether she worked in watercolor or in oils, as she did today.

She glanced around the Bays Arts Co-op Studio & Gallery where she was one of several artists who rented space. More than a cubicle but less than a closed room, each of them had three standing walls on which to hang completed pieces, plus work tables, easels, small display tables, and bins for posters and prints.

Two slots away from the large plate glass window in front, Miranda heard some comings and goings, but paid no attention, lost in her work.

This April, she found herself craving the color yellow. Every touch of it drew her eye, whether of a forsythia bush in bloom, a school bus trundling by, or a bright canary umbrella on someone's balcony.

By training and by inclination, she usually painted from life: from seeing something, seeing *into* it, or studying its surface, or sometimes even seeing *through* it to notice the layer behind, and how that context affected her understanding of the subject. Sunset on clouds, distant hills, tiny grasses less than a foot away, the eyelashes on a big cat, the muscled stance of a buck silhouetted on a ridge. All of it mattered, informed her consciousness, and spoke to her heart.

There were other days when she painted from an inner vision—a close-up detail she hadn't realized she'd noticed, or an "inscape" that began to take form. Today was one of those days. She'd become aware of it this morning, as though puzzle pieces began to assemble. By this afternoon, she knew she'd have no choice but to access the developing image by the most direct route—picking up her paint brush. It'd felt electric today, when brain-met-hand-met-brush-met-paint-met-paintboard.

And most of it was coming out yellow. *Well, I suppose spring itself is pouring through me out onto the paper.* Then, suddenly, it seemed complete. The upper portion of the image was bright, solid blue; the middle, a band of sapphire; the front, a high wall of hundreds of tiny blossoms in bloom, each its own shade of yellow, and all of them iterations of mustard.

It's gotta be in bloom all over the hills south of here. I just have to go see them for myself.

Chapter 2

Meredith had big plans for her Sunday: reading the Sunday *Chronicle*; a decadent brunch at Caravallo, the marvelous cooking school on the far side of the Golden Gate; then home before changing into workout clothes and taking a run. She'd end the day with a facial at her favorite spa, and float off to sleep early in the clean sheets her weekly maid service would by then have smoothed onto her bed.

But first, she'd agreed to meet her mother for lunch on Saturday. Luncheon today would be fun—even if she did suspect her parent had something up her sleeve. They met at The Dining Room, the signature restaurant in the Ritz Carlton on Nob Hill, Mother looking superb in an ochre-colored wool suit, the fabric thin enough to drape and cling fetchingly. The skirt outlined her mother's slim legs, stopping just below the knees; the jacket angled to a diagonal closure with buttons that perfectly matched the chunky amber beads she wore.

Meredith glanced down at her own outfit—navy slacks and a simple navy blazer, her mandarin orange silk blouse offering the only pop of color. *No matter how I try, I'll never match her style.* "Wow, Mom, stunning as always," she said, inhaling the familiar fragrance of Joy.

"Thank you, Meri dear."

Meredith no longer allowed anyone outside the family to call her by her childhood nickname. And her sister felt the same about being called "Mandy" any more. But when it came to parents, how could the child dictate the terms of nomenclature? Meredith had settled for asking her mother not to use the nickname in public. And here, at a private table, it hardly seemed worth arguing the point. She focused as her mother continued her visual inspection and said, "You look . . . well, you look beautiful, but maybe just a little tired."

"Yup, comes with the territory," Meredith said, casting away the criticism before it could sting. Diving behind the menu, she asked, "Did you have something in mind?"

"Hmm," Veri said. "Asparagus soup looks nice. I'll have a cup of that, and the Shrimp Louie salad."

"Perfect," said her daughter. "I'll have the same. So, everything good at home? Dad okay?"

"Oh, yes, your father is fine. If his golf game improves any further, he'll become insufferable."

Meredith smiled. "Better he takes out his frustrations on inanimate objects than on you."

Veri looked up sharply, but then her gaze softened. "You're right, of course. There is always a lot of pressure at work. He handles it well, though."

"Always," Meredith agreed.

The waiter brought them iced waters and warm rolls, then took their order.

"So, to what do I owe the pleasure?" Meredith inquired.

"Can't I just enjoy my elder daughter's company?" Veri asked. Then she paused, as Meredith's gaze bore into hers. "Oh, all right, I do have something to talk with you about," she admitted.

"Thought so."

"It's about that apartment of yours, dear."

Surprised, Meredith halted the bread half-way to her mouth. "I thought you liked it!"

"The view, yes. That much is fabulous. But the building, it's . . . it's cold."

Meredith bit into the warm roll and swallowed before saying, "You're not wrong."

"It seems to me not much thought went into true design or comfort. It's all chrome, glass and concrete. It's . . . sterile. It has no character. It's unsuitable for a young lady of breeding. It's a *nouveau riche* kind of place."

The soup served, Meredith stared down into the pale green swirls. "Well, tell me what you really think, Mother."

"I'm sorry, Meri dear. But you can do better."

"Well, sure, and some day I will. But at this point, this place is exactly on budget. And I have absolutely no time even to think about finding something else."

"And who says you have to do it alone? I could help, you know."

Meredith sighed. "Since we're being blunt today, I

just . . . I want the place to be *mine,* not some fantastic place that's more your taste than something I'd choose myself."

Veri nodded. "You're absolutely right. If I take this on, I'll have to think of you, your likes and dislikes. And of course I wouldn't make any decision without your approval."

"I like the sound of that."

"I'll think of you as a client, not as my daughter. I'll do my best to keep my own feelings separate, I promise."

Meredith sampled the salad. "It couldn't hurt to look," she allowed.

Veri beamed. "Leave it to me."

Charles Jones took a long moment to look into the sapphire-blue eyes of his wife, her beauty still as pleasing to him now as when they'd first met.

His golf game had gone well, and he'd soothed a sore shoulder and hip in their master bath steam shower. Refreshed and ready for a light supper at home, he waited for Veri to finish changing before they headed downstairs.

"How was lunch with Meredith?" he asked, noticing a slight smile tugging at the edges of her mouth. "I take it things went well?"

"Oh, Charles," she exuded. "She agreed to let me look for a place for her!"

He couldn't help but laugh out loud at the youthful exuberance he saw in his wife's face. He noticed her animation often, whether she shared details of one of many charity board meetings or described a shopping spree for one of her select clients. But nothing pleased her more than being able to do something special for her daughters.

Chapter 3

Miranda cranked open the front window of her apartment on Sunday morning, gulping eagerly at the puff of fresh air that wafted inside. She'd opened the rear window first, hoping for a cross-draft that would clear the rooms of residual odors, a peculiar combination of spaghetti sauce and turpentine—one of the reasons she'd been considering switching from oil paints to acrylics, or maybe even concentrating on watercolors.

Ecological impact was another concern. Toxic elements like cadmium, chromium, and lead were used to create pigments, although in minuscule amounts. Oil paints would be the most toxic, using petroleum-based products. Acrylic paint with its polymer base would be less toxic. Watercolor paint would be least toxic of all—a medium she truly enjoyed, but it required quite a different technique and resulted in a particular kind of image, beautiful in its own way but so different from the works of the European masters she'd studied.

Meanwhile, to handle the turpentine odor, she kept a

supply of essential oils handy—a different floral or green for each season, all shipped from her favorite apothecary, Kiehl's, that'd been established in New York in 1851.

Miranda recalled a family trip to New York when she and her sister Meredith had first discovered the store in the East Village. "Oh, Mandy, take a whiff," Meredith had insisted, using her family nickname. Mer had nearly swooned upon inhaling Kiehl's special Musk, declaring that if she ever met a man who wore it, she'd know he was *the one.* Asking the clerk about the tiny bottle of dark glass, they'd been told the founder had developed the signature scent in 1921 and named it Love Oil. "You see my point," her sister had said, peering over her sunglasses as the two of them laughed.

Miranda had found two favorites that day: Moroccan Jasmine to wear, and Rain, which became her go-to fragrance to restore freshness to her surroundings. But before she could pour a tablespoon into her tiny metal fragrance pot and light the votive candle under it, the rooms first had to be cleared of lingering aromas.

She glanced around the apartment. *I could take a walk . . . but I hate to leave the windows open unless I'm home. Not exactly secure.* She decided, instead, to spend a couple of hours cleaning. It would allow her head to clear while she worked, one of her favorite techniques for getting to the bottom of whatever was trying to surface in her mind.

She started in the bathroom, scrubbing the pocked surfaces of the old porcelain tub and sink, carefully wiping the antique mirror, then mopping the mosaic-tiled floor. By comparison, the living-dining area was easy: dusting with a Pledge-infused cloth, vacuuming the cushions of her second-hand sofa, then dry-mopping the hardwood floors.

As she worked, images of the city beyond the walls of her apartment flashed through her mind. Nothing pleased her more than the long walks that were a primary indulgence. Sometimes she hiked the steep hills to marvel at the architectural ingenuity that allowed building on such challenging terrain. Other days she'd stroll through her own artists' area, stepping into other galleries or admiring canvases on display during local street-art events. The Ferry Building sometimes pulled at her, and she'd move from one food kiosk to the next, adding breads and jams, vegetables and grains, to her soon-overburdened basket. And some days she'd call a friend for company and go exploring in the Dogpatch, always finding that a new jazz club or café had sprung up since her last visit.

When she got a travel bug, she often cured it by heading to Chinatown, not only for a scrumptious meal, but to explore treasure-filled shops. Holding in her hand an intricate Japanese *netsuke* carving or standing back to take in the full view of a landscape screen never failed to remind her of the wider world, and of its many artistic interpretations and expressions, from ancient to modern, from classical to avant-garde, from subtle to obvious, and from human subjects to those found in nature.

With pulsing energy, myriad cultures, and endless variety, her home city never failed to inspire. It had pulled at her from across the Bay, beckoning her to leave the suburban beauty of Belvedere and venture to its multicolored streets. It'd called to her sister, too, but Meredith's was a different call, something high-pitched and piercing, something that required hard focus and steely resolve, exhaustive preparation and intense competition.

Miranda felt no sense of competition with other artists, as each creative path was inherently unique. Her own call was toward the thrill of adventure, the wildness of self-expression without approval, the risk of undefined personal failure.

Where learning the game, and playing it better, was Mer's daily challenge, for Miranda, living amongst other creatives was a kind of sanity check, a way to feel reassured she wasn't crazy to spend her time painting canvases no one might buy, enjoy, or even see.

For Miranda, living in the city came at a price. Her rent was too high and her level of interior light too low. Hers was a "garden apartment"—yet the so-called garden at the rear of the property was so steep, it proved impractical, even impossible, to plant anything other than ferns. The deep window-wells allowed her to peer upward toward whatever sunlight might filter through, but the rooms remained dim. Accordingly, she'd made one of them into her bedroom, the other into a cozy living room seldom used except in the evenings.

The front room she configured as her studio, needing

the light to be able to work on her sketches and canvases. It faced a T-intersection, with cross-traffic passing before her large windows, and a street beginning at her front door plummeting downward toward the distant Bay. If she sat at the built-in bench seat near her small foyer, she could catch a glimpse of the water, but this was hardly a "room with a view."

Two hours had passed while Miranda cleaned, putting more vigorous effort into it than usual—a sure sign something was on her mind. She surveyed the results of her work, saw that her modest place now gleamed, and decided she definitely needed to get outside for a while.

Sunday morning, she remembered. *I guess housework was my church service for the day.* "Cleanliness is next to Godliness." She chuckled. The phrase had been hung as a sign in her boarding school.

Slipping into a fleece jacket and pulling on comfortable walking shoes, Miranda closed and secured her windows, grabbed the keys she habitually hung on a hook in the foyer, and headed into the chilly afternoon, locking the front door behind her.

Veri Jones stepped into the kitchen through the garage's connecting door, startling her cook, who'd been singing while she stirred an enormous pot of stew.

"Sorry, Pilar. Mmm, that smells divine!" Stepping to the stove, Veri grabbed a spoon from the adjacent drawer and dipped it into the pot.

"Careful, Madame. Hot!"

Using the spoon's edge to swipe an errant drip from her chin, Veri said "Mmm" again. "And delicious! Where's Mr. Charles?"

"In study, Madame. He play with stamps, but I think he wait for you."

"Dinner at six o'clock?"

Looking as though anything else would unthinkable, Pilar replied affirmatively.

Nodding her agreement, Veri walked the length of the kitchen as she stripped off her coat, then hung it in the foyer closet. She hurried up the wide, arcing staircase, and stepped into her husband's study.

Sensing her presence, he looked up and peered at her over the tops of his glasses. "Uh-oh," he said.

"What?" Veri asked.

"That expression. Looks mighty smug to me. I gather you had success?"

"Oh, Charles," she enthused, kicking off her heels and walking across to the guest chair that faced him across the desk. "Unbelievable." She folded her legs under her and sat. "Remarkable. I did. I found the perfect place."

"And Meredith agrees?"

"Oh, she hasn't seen it yet. Neither has Mandy. But they will. And they'll fall in love with it just as I did."

Charles removed his glasses and, with a small cloth, began to polish the lenses.

"Oh, Charles, what?" Veri asked again.

"You know how you get," he warned, concentrating

on his polishing cloth. "You're over the moon, but you're way ahead of them."

"I'll let them catch up."

He looked up.

"I will!" she insisted.

"Let's have a drink before dinner, and you can tell me all about it."

He folded his glasses, left them on the desk and stood. She picked up her shoes and followed him into their adjacent bedroom suite.

The walk-in closet they shared was the size of a normal bedroom, with wall units that formed alcoves cleverly designed with combinations of hanging bars, shelves, drawers and cubbyholes. On her side of the room, alcoves were ordered by use. In the most distant from the entrance, her formal wear waited as if for the latest invitation, gowns hung beside cubbies showing off satin pumps and sparkling evening purses. The next space held an array of business suits arranged by color, coordinating belts, bags, and scarves, with some hats close at hand. Next stood her collection of casual clothing, where she now stepped into a peach velour at-home set with drawstring pants and a zippered top.

Across the narrow aisle that separated their parallel closet worlds, Charles fussed with the sweater he'd just removed, trying as always to fold it.

"Let me," she said.

Relieved, he pulled on his trusty gray sweats.

She examined the elbows, clucking before commenting, "Looks like we'll need to patch those again. That is, unless I finally have your permission to turn this outfit into rags?"

"These are fine, Dear," he said, patting her fanny affectionately.

"So long as you're comfortable." She smiled up at him, and they made their way downstairs to the den, where they'd have their dinner on trays in front of the television, a cozy fire warming the informal room.

As they savored Pilar's stew, Veri described the house listing her realtor had found, an older home with "good bones" now refurbished with two bedroom suites, and an extra room that could serve as Mandy's studio.

As Pilar removed their trays and brought in mugs of hot tea with freshly baked cookies, Charles munched his treat and seemed to be waiting for his beverage to cool. Veri knew he was deliberating and would talk in a moment.

"Think the two of them can truly cohabit? They're used to their own spaces now, you know. And I scarcely need to point out how different they are." He chose a second cookie and closed his eyes as he savored it.

"No," Veri agreed. "Different as a lynx and a fox."

Charles huffed out a laugh between bites, then posed another question. "If we do this, we're essentially setting her up for this next step in her career. I mean, Mandy has nothing like the resources needed to purchase a home and a studio, whereas Meri . . . is this what we should do? It isn't exactly fair."

"It's life that isn't exactly fair, dear," Veri reflected. "Meri has the money, Mandy doesn't. So what we're really doing is evening out the playing field. " Veri reached for her tea just as her husband reached for his, and the two sipped quietly for a full minute.

"Well," Charles said, "let's hope neither the lynx nor the fox bites us in the—"

"Now, now," she interrupted.

"You do have a talent for finding just the right thing," he offered, patting her thigh just before *Sixty Minutes* began its regularly scheduled broadcast.

Chapter 4

Meredith marched on sturdy high heels down the corridor toward her new office, chin up, but praying not to run into Albert Rothman, not until she'd had a chance to doctor her first cup of coffee and get settled at her desk.

Mercifully, he was nowhere in sight as she poured fresh brew over the half-and-half in the bottom of her office mug, nor did he accost her in the hall. Over the next hour, Meredith lined up the file folders for the day's client projects, met with her assistant Priscilla about upcoming deadlines, and reviewed the report she'd be handing in later in the morning.

Her appointment, scheduled for 11:00 a.m., was with Senior Partner Ron Mansfield, a man she respected and admired, a true mentor who'd always done right by her and other ambitious young members of the firm. Determined not to take advantage of their special friendship, Meredith always turned in top-quality work, and this report would match or exceed her usual standards.

Ron's secretary Joan was a fixture at the firm, having

been with Ron all the way up the ladder. Joan, busy on a phone call, glanced up with a smile for Meredith who approached two minutes before the hour. Joan waved her in, so Meredith, giving Ron's partially open door two courtesy taps, pushed through, then stopped dead in her tracks.

Standing behind Ron's desk was not Ron—but Albert.

"What the—" Meredith began. "What are you doing here?"

"And good morning to you too, Ms. Jones. Ron's been detained. He asked me to—"

"No need," Meredith interrupted. "I'll see Ron later. Thanks anyway."

Meredith turned to leave, but Albert reached the door first and pushed it closed. "I don't think I made myself clear," he said. "Ron *insisted* that I meet with you this morning."

"Why would he do that?" she demanded.

"Why wouldn't he? Rank, and all that."

Meredith suppressed her anger by considering strategies. "Fine," she said after several seconds. "Let me explain it to you."

"No need." Albert reached out for the report, which Meredith held against her chest. But instead of grasping the binder, he grabbed a breast, molding his fingers and palm to its contour like a suction cup.

Shock hit her like a jolt of immobilizing electric current. As rage surged upward, weakening her knees, she managed to stand her ground long enough to push the file at his face.

Taking a step backward, she flung open the door and made a beeline for her office. She locked herself inside, so angry she had to fight the impulse to throw every object on her desk against the nearest wall.

Her hands balled into fists, she stood at her window, trembling at first, and then shaking uncontrollably. *That son of a bitch! Who the hell does he think he is?*

She took deep breaths, wishing Miranda were nearby to run her through a series of Tai Chi exercises. Expletives, retaliatory gestures, half-baked plots flashed like some outrageous MTV video, possibilities skipping like stones flung across the surface of her erratic thoughts.

More deep breaths helped her settle enough to realize she had to think strategically. That was what *he* had done: made a move so bold, so unacceptable, that she *had* to react. What would the only "logical" reaction be? To quit, of course. *That's what he wants: me out of the way. Not only that, he wants to say I quit because I couldn't handle the pressure, the new job was beyond my capabilities. Women were far too emotional to hold down a job at this level. Yes, that's what he wants. Well, hell will freeze over before I give him the satisfaction.*

A chill ran down her spine as though icy fingers reached at her from a place inside she hadn't known existed.

Miranda climbed the steep sidewalk toward her apartment, relishing the exercise while being mindful of the cultural shifts from block to block.

She'd enjoyed a long stroll downhill toward the Bay, and a leisurely stay sipping hot tea in a café with a view, even making a few quick sketches in the small pad she always carried in a slim, zippered fanny pack. While golden afternoon light bounced off high glass and low water, she headed home.

The café had been in the Dogpatch—a long, narrow strip of land on the east side of the city—developed more than a hundred years ago as an enclave of cottages and flats for workers along with shipyards commercial buildings as the area first began to industrialize.

Potrero Hill, the adjacent neighborhood, appealed both for its typically sunny days away from the chill fog across town to the west and for its glorious views of the Bay. Having started as a Caucasian working class neighborhood in the 1850s, it began attracting working professionals in the 1990s. In the interim, the 1960s had seen an influx of artists who lived in some spaces, and transformed others into studios and galleries.

Progressing westward, next came the Mission District, with a higher mix of Hispanic residents and generally lower rents. But the 1990s gentrification of Potrero had also spilled into the Mission, with friction sometimes understated and sometimes aggressive. Miranda had even seen a sign advocating that "natives" eradicate Yuppies by vandalizing their cars.

Huffing a little as she headed up the last block toward her apartment, Miranda zipped her fleece higher against the early evening chill. She crested the hill, glanced at her building's front door, and reached into her pocket for her keys. She was wondering what to do about dinner, when a man seemed to leap out of nowhere.

Startled, she stepped back to let him pass, but he began shouting and poking a finger toward her chest. "You got no right to be here!" he yelled. "You're the ones driving up our rents, till the good people can't even live here no more!"

Alarmed, Miranda steadied her breath and bent her knees while she assessed him. His eyes seemed wild with agitation, his clothes unkempt and his body language aggressive.

"What?! You gonna Kung Fu me?" he demanded.

"Just trying to get home," she said quietly.

"Yeah, well, get the hell back to where you came from!"

He began to advance, and Miranda, drawing automatically on her years of study, began performing the smooth motion of a classic Tai Chi step-back-block.

"Now what're you doin'? You're circling and flapping your arms like some crazy-ass bird!"

Miranda had now put enough distance between the man and herself to get away—by running, or maybe just by jogging. She kept him in sight for another few steps, then turned and did a fast-walk to the end of her block.

"We know where you live!" he shouted. "We want you out!" Though he continued yelling after her, he didn't pursue. And while she circumnavigated her entire block, she steadied her breath and brought her heart rate back to something resembling normal. She paused when she came near her building again, but the man had vanished, and she let herself in.

"Holy crap!" she said aloud, once she'd locked herself inside. Her hands shook as she double-checked the locks on all her windows. They still shook as she turned the water on for a hot bath.

She'd left her parents' home in search of her own. She'd thought this was a good, solid start. Now she began to wonder whether the movement she felt was an earthquake building deep underground.

Chapter 5

Veri Jones looked at her reflection in the foyer mirror and burst out laughing.

"What's so funny?" her husband asked, his voice booming from the dining room.

"Nothing, dear," she called back.

She heard his footsteps and the rattle of his newspaper as he headed in her direction. "Just happy, then?"

She smiled at her husband. "You know me too well, Charles."

"I do, in fact. Meetings with a realtor and a daughter? A banner day, I'd say."

"There you have it," she confirmed.

When Charles drew close enough, she rose even higher on her pumps and bussed him lightly so as not to smudge the red lipstick she favored.

"Have a large time," he said.

"I plan to."

Veri drove slowly through the neighborhood where she'd be meeting the realtor, noting that about half the historic three- or four-story town homes had been renovated. Power lines criss-crossed overhead, cars lined both sides of the streets, and an occasional ficus tree managed to survive in its concrete footing. The street angled up from sea-level—not as steeply as some in this city of hills— but enough that the building probably did offer views.

As she parked, she caught sight of Mrs. Rimaldi at the front door. After quick pleasantries, the realtor opened the lockbox, retrieved keys, and let herself and her pro- spective client into the home. The two women stood in the foyer and Veri could hardly keep herself from begin- ning their walk-through to see how accurate the descrip- tions had been.

This would be the ninth property she'd inspected with Mrs. Rimaldi, and she'd nearly despaired of find- ing something that would work. This one, however, had sounded good over the phone, and she'd tried not to feel that its location on Jones Street signified destiny.

Veri checked her watch. "My daughter Meredith will arrive in about half an hour, but I want to see it for my- self, first, to get a sense of how the space would fit for her and her sister."

The realtor nodded. "Two girls, both professional?"

"Yes," Veri agreed. "One works in the financial district."

"That's practically next door, easiest commute pos- sible," the realtor pointed out.

"Right," Veri affirmed. "The other will work at home."

"So, location is no problem. Does she have one of

those brand new computer jobs? Telecommuting, I believe they call it."

"Oh, no, nothing like that. She's an artist."

The realtor looked confused. "Uh-huh," she said, fixing her smile back in place. Then, as though a light bulb switched on in the woman's brain, she said, "Oh, this location makes total sense! The Academy of Art University's studios and classrooms are right here!"

"Honestly, I hadn't known about that. But I've always thought of Russian Hill as a good neighborhood," Veri offered. Then she added, "You do still agree, don't you? I want my girls to feel safe in their new home."

"Oh, they *will*," the realtor reassured her, "even though it does include the famous 'crookedest street in the world.'" The woman's soprano laugh grated on Veri's nerves, and she hid her grimace with a forced smile.

"They'll need separate bedrooms—bedroom suites with their own bathrooms would work best."

"Exactly, and when you told me you needed a two-roommate configuration, I wanted to show you this property," the realtor enthused.

"Seems very unusual for a Victorian to have two upstairs bathrooms," Veri remarked.

"Well, first, they're not both upstairs. Second, this Victorian was completely renovated, permits and all."

Veri pursed her lips. "That must come with a hefty price tag."

"See, that's the beauty of this listing. The previous owners spent several years wrangling with the city, sub-

mitting plans, having them rejected, then revised, and finally approved. But by the time they got their approvals
and had the work completed, something else happened.
I think he was transferred to an overseas job. In any case,
they have to sell quickly, so they've dropped the price
significantly."

Veri felt her spirits lift. "Excellent! Let's have a look."

"Now this main floor has a newly done kitchen-and-
dining, then the living room, and the den. Well, in the old
days, this would've been the parlor."

"I see," Veri said, following the realtor in a circle, "with
the double staircase in the middle of the main floor."

"Right. And up here, we have a master suite."

The stairs led them to a sunny apartment with a spacious bedroom and lovely bathroom, the mosaic tiles
reminiscent of the home's original style.

"Meredith would love this!" she exclaimed. "Look at
the views! The Golden Gate out one window, a slice of the
Bay Bridge out the other!"

"Yes, spectacular," the realtor said with a dreamy
voice.

"Uh, but where's the other bedroom?"

"Follow me." The two descended past the main floor
into a basement. "Now here's a second master suite, you
might say."

"Wonderful windows, plenty of sunlight," Veri said.

"This space is a little more segmented," the realtor
explained. "I mean, the bedroom is smaller, and so is the

bath, but then there's a separate room. You said your other daughter works at home?"

"She does," Veri confirmed.

"Perfect, because this could be her office. Or, rather, her studio, I suppose."

"It's quite suitable," Veri remarked more to herself than to the other woman as her own thoughts swirled with tangible possibilities. Veri hardly noticed the grin that spread across the realtor's face.

Meredith announced her arrival with a "hello?" from the main floor. Forty-five minutes later, Veri and Meredith had completed their joint walk-through with Mrs. Rimaldi, and the realtor had stepped away to give them privacy.

"Good bones, as you would say, Mother."

"Exactly."

"And that view from the upstairs bedroom . . . well, the views are actually better than what I have now."

"They just might be," Veri replied, doing her best to keep her tone neutral. *If I'm too enthusiastic, Meredith will feel pushed.*

"But, Mother, this is too big for one person! I wouldn't know what to do with that huge downstairs. You weren't thinking I'd take a roommate at this late date, were you?"

Veri inhaled, exhaled, then asked, "Would you consider sharing the place with your sister?"

Meredith looked startled, then concerned. "Does she know about this?"

"No, dear, I'm asking you first."

Meredith seemed to relax a notch at that news, but then said, "It's moot, really. She can't afford it."

"Well, perhaps your father and I could make up the difference for a while."

"She'll never agree," Meredith snapped.

"She doesn't have to know, does she? I imagine the rental agency will require a credit history beyond what Miranda could demonstrate at this point."

Meredith chewed her lip. "I . . . well, that's really not up to me, that's between you and Mandy."

"The thing is, she'd be safer, Meredith dear. So would you. I stay awake at night worrying."

Meredith looked at her mother and smiled. "You'll do that anyway, Mom."

Veri smiled back. "Well, you know what I mean."

Meredith sighed. "*If* she accepts your terms, and *if* she likes the place, there's one more thing."

"What's that?"

"She can't paint in here. I couldn't stand the smell."

Veri crossed her arms. "She *will* paint, Meredith dear. But not on the two upper floors. She'll have that extra room downstairs, with a door and a window. That'll be her studio. The fumes will be contained."

Meredith nodded her head, then followed her mother outside, where the realtor waited.

"Thank you so much, Mrs. Rimaldi. I'm not sure whether this will work quite yet. We'll need to discuss it with the family and I'll get back to you."

After the cordialities were exchanged with the realtor, as well as quick hugs with Meredith, Veri climbed into her car. *I'll call the realtor and see if I can talk her down a bit, maybe arrange a lease option. And get her to add a lock to the front door, do the floors, and give it a fresh coat of paint.*

There was no doubt in her mind that her plan to keep her daughters safe, happy, and close, was well under way.

Part II
1995

"Fine art is that in which the hand, the head and the heart go together."

– John Ruskin

Chapter 6

Miranda raised her voice. "That's right, Kathryn. You tell Starfleet they're wrong. Oh, but you can't, because you're stuck in the Delta quadrant!"

Talking back to the television screen was nothing new for Miranda, when Kathryn Janeway filled it. As a female Captain of a starship, she struck an excellent balance between authority and compassion, patience and determination, courage and passion.

But where the Starship captain had the advantage of a holodeck—a virtual suite where anything imaginable could be programmed and experienced—Miranda had only the raw materials at hand.

What kind of space would she create with unlimited time, and money? Probably something like the imaginary Leonardo da Vinci studio the writers of *Voyager* had envisioned: a cavernous room with high ceilings, large tables, easels holding canvases in various stages of completion, and an inspiring sense of beautiful chaos. Yes, some truly artistic space with plenty of order so supplies were readily at hand. But, unlike Master da Vinci's, she'd want hers to be more rustic, more closely tied to nature.

Then she looked around, ashamed not to be more grateful for where she'd landed. The home she now shared with her sister was the envy of all their friends. Her parents had even signed the lease agreement, since she'd never have qualified on her own. Now she spent a small fortune on rent, but the lease-to-purchase option meant some day she and Meredith could split the proceeds if and when they wanted to sell and go their separate ways.

Her downstairs suite had three times the light of her old place, and gave her access to a beautiful main floor kitchen-dining-living area she shared with her sister. She entertained a lot less than Meredith did, and sometimes found herself banished to the "basement." But one woman's basement was another woman's castle, she reminded herself. Her lovely bedroom suite was large enough to comfortably hold her queen-sized bed, end tables and a chest of drawers, on which rested her own small TV. And her studio space was so peaceful and quiet that she'd now finished several paintings she'd decided not to work on in the Co-op's shared studio.

The financial arrangements at her new home still bothered her, in that she knew her mother had co-signed the lease agreement to help her—help she was quite sure Meredith hadn't needed.

"That just means Meredith got a better deal, and so

did you," their mother had explained. Meredith remained mute on the subject, dismissive if the topic ever arose.

Well, such was life as the less successful daughter in the Jones family. Meredith had been pulling down some sort of astronomical salary for several years, and for the most part seemed to love her work. Yet Miranda knew the pressures of her job could be crushing.

Now some of that pressure had landed on *her*, enough that Miranda took some commercial work she'd hoped to avoid. But creating the art work for ad campaigns paid high fees, and when these opportunities came along, she was in no position to decline.

Her mother always seemed more proud of Miranda's original work than of any work-for-hire, and attended every showing, no matter how unglamorous the gallery. Her father, however, only seemed to show interest when he could point to a glossy magazine full-page ad share-able with his golf buddies.

Maybe he'll approve of me one day. Maybe he won't. That'll be up to him. Not my problem. She repeated that parental mantra as often as necessary.

As for approval from her sister, that was always an enigma. Mostly, her sibling just seemed too busy to con-sider anything beyond her own responsibilities. But during all-too-rare occasions, the two would have a real heart-to-heart about life, love, and the pursuit of happi-ness that would restore her faith in the notions of both family and friendship.

Something seemed vaguely uncomfortable between them since they'd become roommates. At first, they'd each been too preoccupied with the move to discuss anything but logistics. Then, once they were truly settled, they were off to the races with work.

Had they been closer when they'd lived separately? Perhaps. Time together, then, had seemed more precious, and they'd saved up their stories and confidences. Now, they rarely had time for one another.

Miranda had tried for an impromptu breakfast this morning by cooking French toast. But her sister, often a sound sleeper, hadn't stirred. So Miranda'd enjoyed one piece herself, then had taken the rest to her neighbor Max, who always seemed grateful for her small offerings.

No problem, she thought as she cleaned the kitchen. *That's why I planned tonight's dinner for us. It'll be such fun, like old times!*

So how long would this chapter of life last? How long would she and her oh-so-different sister enjoy sharing a home? And what kind of home would Miranda really want, if and when it was time to leave this one?

It all seemed so daunting: imagineering a different kind of life than the one she now lived in San Francisco. *If only I could paint what I want, and then step into it,* she mused. *That would be perfect.*

Meredith opened one eye, peered out the window at the fog, then closed her eye again. Having treated herself to high-thread-count sheets for her new house a few months earlier, she took advantage of the delicious comfort they offered to slip back into sleep.

When the aromas of French toast wafted up the stairs and slid under her door, they moved right into her dream, rather than waking her.

Two hours later, when she did finally awaken, she overheard the dim sound of the dishwasher. *Mandy's cleaning again. Sometimes it's like living with a maid.*

The vague guilt she felt fled when her private line rang. Reaching to her bedside table for the handset, she offered a sleepy "Hello?"

"Hey, Meredith, still in bed?" Her friend Brian's voice sounded entirely too wide awake.

"Wouldn't you like to know?" she sassed.

"So, hey, wanna go sailing today?"

"In the pea soup? Absolutely not."

"Yeah, you're right. Sun is supposed to come out later."

"So call me then," Meredith rejoined, ready to hang up.

"So, okay, how about brunch?" he offered.

"You're on, if it's Dutch treat."

"Suits me. Usual place?"

"Sure. See you in . . ." Meredith glanced at her clock, which read 10:30. ". . . in forty-five?"

"Yup."

Meredith took the quickest shower she could manage, twisted her hair into a knot and covered it with her favorite blue baseball cap, yanked on jeans, a T-shirt, blazer, socks and running shoes, then grabbed her purse before heading downstairs.

"Hey, Mandy. Have a nice day," she barely had time to say before heading to the garage.

She didn't stop long enough to hear her sister's reply.

Miranda shouted "Don't forget dinner!" after her sister, but wondered whether her words had been heard. She didn't doubt, however, that Meredith had put their plans for a Sunday meal in her Palm Pilot, as she did every commitment.

Miranda glanced out the window and watched Meredith's BMW roar down the street. The May Gray outside made their home seem all the more cozy, and a perfect day for creating first a meal, then a new painting project.

The meal would be dinner, but she mentally listed it first because she'd use her slow cooker. Though she rarely ate meat, somehow serving a comfort-food Sunday dinner seemed a nice way to warm up the chilly day, and connect with her sister.

She'd bought a roast, which she pulled from the fridge, along with the carrots she'd chop into bite-sized pieces. With these items placed on a large cutting board, she knelt to reach into the back of a lower cabinet to retrieve her trusty slow cooker and her largest skillet.

New potatoes filled a small basket on her counter. She washed them, placed them in the bottom of her pot, then chopped and added the carrots. When she'd minced two cloves of garlic she sautéed them in olive oil. Next she unwrapped the meat and placed it to sear in the hot pan as enticing aromas swirled through the kitchen.

The sizzling reminded her that Meredith liked to fix stir-fry. *Perfect for her. Quick, decisive, pungent, complex.* Miranda laughed out loud at how well that described not only Meredith's cooking, but the woman herself.

So how would I describe my own culinary style? Slow, deliberate, flavorful, simple. Miranda turned the meat in the pan as she pondered that self-description. Whether cooking or painting, it was true her work required patience and time to develop. *Yes, that fits.* But what about simplicity? *Not so sure about that. Meredith appears complicated, and she is! Maybe I appear simple, but am I? No, not really.*

For her to call her sister complex and not recognize that quality in herself would be . . . the pot calling the kettle black.

Chapter 7

Miranda knew the main floor of her home must now be fragrant with cooking aromas, but she could only smell paint.

With Meredith likely out for several hours, and the fumes masked by the savory meal under way, today had been a perfect opportunity to add character to her walls.

Before moving in, she'd carefully chosen pleasing background colors for her future wall murals. While professional house painters had tackled the second and third floors, she'd asked that they only do base coats on the first level.

Meanwhile, she'd mapped out her own plans for wall murals. Her basic theme was to "extend" the views the home actually offered. She would treat each wall as if it were transparent, and their home were not surrounded by other buildings. So she would paint *in* some elements—like the bridges— but paint *out* others.

To research her imagined perspective, she'd spent time sketching in what was now Meredith's third-floor suite, drawing "downward" to sloping streets, level water, and the lower structures of the immense bridges—some of which would actually be visible from their house.

Her studio, with a north-facing window, also had a large, blank wall that, if she could see through it, would offer the Bay Bridge view eastward. She'd already completed a simple three-piece mural: pale blue sky for the upper half, cloud bank filling one quarter of the image below the sky, and gray-blue water for the lower quarter.

Today, referring to her sketches, she penciled, then painted in, one of the steel-gray cross-hatched vertical pillars bisecting the center of her wall. Its top disappeared beyond the upper edge of the mural, but from it, the suspension cables draped right and left; at its mid-point the sturdy deck flew straight across the image. And the massive pillar seemed to float on the water below.

Miranda put down her paint brush, rolled her shoulders, then moved aside her step ladder. Standing back far enough to see the whole wall, she nodded, smiled, then sighed.

The soft grays and blues lent the room a peaceful quality. Yet the forces within the bridge image represented tremendous energy. *Tension in the cables; compression in the pillars.* That's what her research had revealed, and sure enough, the image seemed to deliver a mighty sense of understated power.

And that'd been her plan: that the studio would be both a haven and an energy source to fuel the engine of her work.

She crossed her arms and glanced out the actual

window. Then she giggled. The real view of water and bridge peeking through buildings she pretended not to see, aligned marvelously with her newly painted one. Though this couldn't be called a true *trompe-l'oeil*, the mural would fool the eye for at least a moment or two. If nothing else, this would be a fun image, one to place the viewer at the center of an imagined building with fewer neighbors—even if she herself were the only one who ever saw it.

Miranda already knew the mural she'd planned for her north-and-west–facing bedroom would include an "imagineered" view of the Golden Gate, but it would have to wait for another day. By the time she'd finished the studio wall, cleaned the brushes and put away her supplies, it was four o'clock—time to check the roast, set the table, then take a shower and get into comfy but nice at-home clothes.

She'd kept the large studio sliding window open all day to make sure fumes didn't accumulate, and now she detected no trace in the kitchen. Indeed, the upper floor was redolent with divine cooking smells.

She inserted the chick flick she'd rented for them from Blockbuster, the perfect entertainment for their girls' night in.

She'd considered *Sleepless in Seattle*, released a couple of years earlier. She'd also thought about the new movie *Clueless*, thinking it'd be great to spend the evening laughing. In the end, she chose *Pretty Woman*, the closest thing to a modern-day *Cinderella* story—in some ways the farthest thing from their own lives, absent as they were of romance; in some ways their story held the kind of magical privilege others only dreamt might happen to them.

An hour later, the slow cooker had clicked off, the roast and vegetables done to perfection, but Meredith hadn't arrived, nor had she called to say she was running late.

Miranda waited another hour before slicing the meat and fixing herself a plate. She sat alone at their kitchen dining table, rather than using one of the trays she'd prepared, doing her best to enjoy the excellent food.

When she'd finished, she washed her dishes, wondering whether to keep a plate warm for her missing sister. But it now seemed late enough that it was unlikely she'd want food when she got home, so Miranda located appropriately sized storage containers and put away the leftovers.

She'd bought their favorite Häagen Dazs flavors for dessert—Rum Raisin for Mer, Butter Pecan for herself. So she served up a bowl, hit it with a light drizzle of warmed chocolate fudge, and settled herself in front of the television. The movie, which she'd seen before, was even better this time, and she marveled at the seemingly effortless skill with which Julia Roberts transformed herself from rags to riches, then held to her dignity so fiercely that Richard Gere seemed to have no choice but to become her Prince Charming.

Miranda was giving the kitchen a final polish when she heard the garage door open, and couldn't help but glance at the clock, which read 9:10 p.m. *It's April Fool's Day, and I'm the fool.*

"God, something smells good!" Meredith declared as she pushed through the front door. "Oh! Did I forget? I did! I forgot! I had sushi with Brian. Sorry, Kiddo. I'm beat and I have an early morning. Night!"

Miranda watched as her sister climbed up to the third floor, then said to the empty room, "Good night."

Chapter 8

Miranda sat at her favorite café in the Dogpatch. Even though she now lived farther away than she had at her old apartment, she still enjoyed the comfort of familiar surroundings. Clocks had jumped forward an hour during the night, and she'd gotten an early start so as not to feel the loss of time. Today she even relished the fog that, for once, had swirled down even to this part of the city.

With the usual Bay view shrouded, she turned more easily to an inner view. Fragrant steam rose from a mug of Earl Grey next to her, and her pencil began to move across a fresh page in the small sketchbook she'd pulled from her fanny pack.

A coastal view began to emerge—such a constant theme that it held no surprise at first. Rugged escarpment topped with windswept pines; waves rushing toward shore from an agitated sea; cottages peeking between thick tree trunks.

At first she thought she'd sketched the cliffs near Stinson Beach, long a favorite destination. As a Marin County native, she knew the beautiful sweep of coastline well, and had over the years enjoyed long walks on its sands as well as solitary sessions with her watercolor journal. After working, she'd treat herself to tasty fried calamari at the Sand Dollar Restaurant that'd first opened its doors in 1921. With the drive back only forty-five minutes to the family home, Stinson made for a restorative day trip.

But as she considered the image more carefully she realized several features didn't match. First, the hills were much closer to the coastline. Second, clusters of tall trees topped the hills and ran down into small valleys, not a feature at Stinson. *More like Big Sur . . . but I almost never drive south.* Third, the curved escarpment held a taller structure . . . a tower partially obscuring a house. The imaginary place held as much mystery as her childhood castles.

Had she ever driven home from farther up the coast? Yes, she'd driven south from Portland once, passing through the Sinkyone Wilderness, but that area was remote and desolate. Her sketch showed the rooftops of a little town winking through pine trees. Though the image lived vividly in her imagination, she couldn't remember a real place she'd seen that combined those particular elements.

Leaving this small mystery for now, she flipped through the pages of the sketchbook and noticed how many times she'd penciled the view from this very spot: the Bay Bridge arcing off toward Oakland—a gray behemoth that seemed as gracefully airborne as a whale mid-breach; the great ships plying these active waters, proving the city's worth in trade, demonstrating its international connections with flags and vessel names.

There were sketches from other vantage points as well: the Transamerica from Meredith's old apartment; the vantage point from under the Golden Gate, structures crowded to water's edge as though waiting for embarkation; glancing views of the skyline from office buildings, freeways, bridges. Her city was like no other ... and like *all* others: suffocatingly compressed and ingeniously engineered, carefully planned, and haphazardly overgrown.

But where, in all these artist snapshots, were the glimpses of nature she craved? Where were the wild creatures she studied, the landscapes she adored, the actual subjects of the paintings that now added up to her personal brand and growing reputation? The omission hit her like a tidal wave. This sketchbook was as clear a picture of her day-to-day life as could be captured. Yet from it were missing the core images of her career, the elements that spoke to her heart.

Would she need to escape from her physical home to find her heart-home? This conflict at the core felt suddenly dangerous and destructive, as if magma were pressuring the mantle, looking for a vulnerable place to blow as hot and wild as a volcano.

The cozy café session and the long walk to and from hadn't soothed her as it usually did. Once home, she removed the new sketch from its booklet and placed it in a frame on her work table. *Where is this place?* She still didn't know, nor could she discern what it might signify, but the agitation signaled a message, and she knew better than to ignore it.

Meredith both loved and hated her new home. Well, to be fair, there was nothing about the house she didn't love. It was the situation that continued to make her uncomfortable.

I'm just too old to have a roommate, she thought irritably. *Here I am afraid to go downstairs to do laundry, lest I run into Miranda and hurt her feelings. Again.*

Her sister meant well. Her sister was a damn saint by anyone's standards. Kind, generous, patient, thoughtful, Mandy never missed an opportunity to bring home something her big sister might enjoy for dinner, or put a charming bunch of fresh flowers on the dining table. The kitchen was always clean. The whole house was always clean. The dreaded paint fumes had never materialized, at least while Meredith was on the premises.

As Meredith pulled her Beamer into traffic, she shook her head because here was one more thing to add to her guilty-list. Meredith was heading to their parents' for dinner, and Miranda wasn't invited.

Veri threw open the front door, gave her elder daughter a fierce hug, then held her at arm's length for the customary inspection.

"You look good, dear. Almost."

Meredith winced at the near-compliment. "Thanks, I think."

Veri closed the door behind them and led the way toward the den, where her husband stood as they entered.

"Well, look what the cat dragged in," said Charles, tossing aside his newspaper and giving Meredith a bear hug. "Something to drink?"

"Absolutely," Meredith answered, sinking into one of the comfortable arm chairs.

"Pinot?" her mother asked.

Meredith nodded, then accepted the offered glass and closed her eyes as the first chilled sip slid down her throat. "That's better," she remarked unnecessarily.

"So. How's life in the Big City?" her father inquired jovially.

"Good! Mostly. Very good financially. Which mostly makes it worth all the aggravation."

"Stress is not a joke, Meri dear," her mother warned. "I doubt you do nearly enough to ease all the tension."

The three sat in companionable silence for a few moments, and Meredith took a deep breath. Glancing around the familiar room, she noted the exquisite furnishings her mother had carefully assembled, realizing with some surprise what a long way she herself still had to go to achieve her parent's style and taste. "Such a lovely room, Mother."

"Thank you, dear."

Meredith noted the slight flush of pleasure that briefly colored her mother's face.

"How are things at the Jones sisters' homestead?" her father asked.

"Oh, the place is fantastic," Meredith gushed. "Mother really worked her magic this time. It's perfect. I have to pinch myself when I'm in my bedroom. The last time I priced a home that offered views of both bridges, it topped five million!"

Charles chortled.

Veri looked embarrassed, adding, "Money isn't everything, you know."

"No, but it's *something*." The sentence was uttered simultaneously, the father and daughter speaking as echoes of one another.

All three of them laughed. Then Veri said, "How is Mandy getting along?"

"Fine, as far as I can tell. She's busy. We hardly even see each other, really. Between my work schedule and her . . . well I suppose she's working, too. We don't . . . have much overlap."

Charles chose this moment to retreat to his abandoned newspaper, while Veri regarded her daughter with interest. "You're not having man trouble, are you? I mean, getting in each other's way because—"

"God, no!" Meredith exclaimed. "Who has time for boyfriends? Well, I can only speak for myself of course, but I've seen no evidence of . . . well, you know, no trace that she's had male visitors any more than I have."

"You girls might invite your parents over for dinner,

you know," Veri complained. "I haven't even seen the place since Mandy did that mural. Is it nice?"

"It's . . . amazing. I mean, it's strange. It's unusual. No one else would have thought of it."

"Why? Did she paint a jungle scene with monkeys swinging from trees?" her father asked, his barbed words a contrast to his innocent expression.

"Charles!" Veri scolded.

Meredith laughed. "No, nothing like that. It's more like a giant architectural rendering."

Her father's eyebrows shot up. "Really? How so?"

"It's the bottom of the bridge."

"Why would you paint the bottom? I don't understand." Her father scowled.

"It's as if she looked at the east view from my room, then imagined what it'd look like two stories down. If the wall wasn't there."

"Oh, my," her mother said breathlessly. "Only Mandy."

Meredith looked into her mother's eyes, seeing there the glow of admiration she never quite saw for her own achievements.

"Brilliant," Veri added quietly.

"Well, if it's all that *brilliant*, we'll have to arrange a viewing, I suppose." Charles's comment may have been a compliment technically, but to Meredith it sounded more like a growl.

"The fog is terrible tonight, dear. And besides, we've lost an hour with Daylight Savings. Why don't you stay the night? You know your room is always ready. Tomorrow you can get an early start and beat the traffic in from Belvedere."

"Thanks, Mom. I did bring a change of clothes, just in case. I think I will. I'm really tired."

Meredith had to admit the dinner of homemade bouilla-base with crusty, hot bread prepared by the family's marvelous cook was superb, as always. After a dessert of sorbet and Milano cookies, Pilar said she'd bring decaf lattes to the sitting room. Charles built a small fire against the chilly evening, but then said he'd be heading up to read in bed.

"We'll be up in a little while, dear," Veri said.

When the hot drinks had been served, Meredith reached for hers and tucked her feet, covering them with the throw draped over the edge of her chair.

"Ready to talk about it, now that your father's gone upstairs?" Veri asked, coming right to the point.

Meredith sighed. "I guess so. It's . . . well, I was going to say it's Mandy, but that's too simple. It's . . . we just seem to be oil and water."

"Always have been, dear. Different as salt and sugar."

Meredith pursed her lips. "I suppose that makes me the salty one, since she's always so sweet."

"I'd say so," Veri confirmed, a note of kindness in her voice. "Salt of the earth, Meri. Makes the world go round."

Meredith barked an unamused laugh. "And you catch more flies with sugar," she quipped.

"Platitudes aside, what's causing the friction?"

"She's too sweet! She's too perfect! But on the other hand, she's never seems to *do* anything! I mean, I work my *ass* off, and every time I come home, there she sits!"

"Language, Meredith."

"I'm sorry, Mom. But what am I supposed to think? I don't know exactly what your financial arrangement is, but how can I say nothing when you're paying through the nose for that incredible house?"

"Ah. The Prodigal."

"What's that supposed to mean? Am I going to get a lecture now about forgiving and forgetting?"

"Oh, Meri. There's nothing to forgive! Your sister is doing her life her way. You're doing your life your way, and it's just perfect. *You* are just perfect, exactly as you are. For now. The friction, well . . . it's like an emery board that'll smooth off your rough edges as you go."

Meredith sagged in her chair. "I'm too exhausted for metaphors at this point, Mother. And I'm too worried about the financial disparity to just let it slide."

Veri sighed and put down her coffee cup. She steepled her fingers for a moment—a sure indication she was preparing some pronouncement. Meredith shrank further into the cushions.

"I used to think exactly the way you and your father do about money," she began. "I think it's all the years on the G.B. Ballet board that's helped me see things in a different light. You see, things are different for artists."

"Yeah, they can't—or won't—pay their bills!"

"Sadly, that is sometimes true, even at Greater Bay. And there are artists who allow themselves to slide into a victim mentality, a sense that the world owes them for being who they are, doing what they do."

"Exactly!"

"There are other artists, though, who struggle every day to balance what they see inside with what they see outside."

"Well, great. We *all* have to strike that balance. Everyone I know puts in the hard work and the responsibilities first, then if there's anything left over, they try to smooth themselves out."

"Yes. And could you do that if you lived with the constant pressure of images trying to paint themselves inside your head? What do you think Shakespeare did when the iambic pentameter started strafing through his mind? How did Mark Rothko even walk from room to room with those huge canvases shadowing his steps?"

"Seriously? You're putting my little sister on a par with some of the world's greatest artists?"

Veri took another deep breath. "Their greatness only appeared later. It was what they had to *live* with that I'm talking about. I've known an artist or two who tried to suppress it all. It can turn very ugly."

Meredith could feel the frown crease her forehead.

"I'm sorry, dear. I really didn't mean to lecture. I guess the only thing I really want to say is that your sister does work hard. I know you'll find this difficult to believe, but in her own way, she works as hard as you do."

Meredith felt her face heat with irritation.

"What if you could consider what I said as a theory? What if it were *theoretically* true that your sister is working hard, and might one day surprise us with unexpected success, even if it's financially modest? Would you allow that might be possible?"

After a long pause, Meredith said, "Yes. I guess so."

"Then do, dear daughter. Make that allowance. Even if only for your mother."

Meredith lifted her gaze to see the love in her mother's eyes that she'd craved for so long. For tonight, perhaps that was enough.

Chapter 9

Miranda awoke Monday morning excited about working on her second mural.

She took portable painting supplies to the garage and put them in the trunk of her car. Since Meredith's car wasn't there, she concluded her sister had spent the night elsewhere. *Where? Wish I knew! But she'll tell me when she's ready.*

With her sister not around for breakfast, Miranda made herself a bowl of oatmeal, a slice of cinnamon raisin toast, and a mug of tea. While she sipped the hot brew, she jotted down a list of what else she'd need for today's outings.

First, she'd stop by the Co-op Studio to see what paintings might have sold, restock some basics, and make sure her space was in order.

Then she'd head toward the Golden Gate Park and find a safe place for her car. She'd put sketching and watercolor supplies in her backpack so she could hike, looking for the best lower-views of the big red bridge. She also packed her camera, thinking she might need to examine the site from several different angles to get the right one for her second mural.

Miranda had always thought the name play clever: Bays Arts Co-op Studio & Gallery brought to mind *Beaux Arts* while also referencing its Bay Area location.

The Studio-Gallery looked like exactly what it was: a working studio for busy artists. It had neither the glitz nor the polish that the high end galleries offered. But though she did sometimes enjoy soaking up the rarefied atmosphere of multi-thousand-dollar canvases carefully hung and illuminated in sleek white rooms, she also found those settings could drain the warmth from a painting, leaving it adrift in a remote sea of ice, out of context and only appreciated for its monetary value. Here the work could be seen in the context of the effort that produced it—blood, sweat and tears inclusive.

Miranda bustled into her own work space and began moving paint cans, jars of brushes, and easels. Then as she worked her way through a bin containing some of her prints, she glanced up to see her colleague Wesley Adams.

"Hey, Wesley," she said.

"Yeah. Hey, Miranda."

Since his voice held a note of irritation, she stopped what she was doing and asked, "Everything good?"

He stood a short distance away, tall and gangly, a half-grown beard partially concealing a pock-marked complexion.

"Since you asked, no. Not really."

"Oh. Sorry to hear that," she said. *I really don't want to get drawn into one of Wesley's dramas today!*

"Are you? Well, you should know."

What the—? Doing her best to hide her own irritation, she said, "I'm not sure what you mean. But I'd be happy to meet you one day next week for a cup of tea and talk about it."

"Tea? Yeah, I don't think so. Not my cup o', if you know what I mean."

"Okay. Well, I have someplace to be soon, so I can't visit very long today."

"Oh, we don't need to *visit,* Miranda. I think we've already done quite enough of *that.*"

The bitter edge to his tone caught her up short.

"I have no idea what's bothering you, Wesley. I'm sorry you're having a bad day. Excuse me."

"There's no excuse for you!" the man said with enough heat to scorch the painting he'd been holding while they'd been talking.

Miranda took a closer look at her colleague, then took a step back. *Something's wrong with him. I don't even feel safe. I can't believe this is happening again . . . with someone I know!*

She wondered for a moment whether Wesley was going to echo the same refrain the angry resident had hollered, claiming she didn't belong in the neighborhood. Instead, she listened bewildered as he continued his tirade.

"You *know* what you've been doing. You've been

poaching my work. I've spent a small fortune—money I didn't even have—to travel to State Parks. I've been creating these beautiful paintings. And what do I find when I get back? I look through your paintings, and you've been copying mine!"

"Copying?!" She could feel heat suffuse her face and her eyes widen in disbelief. But when she tried to speak, no sound would come out of her mouth.

"You know I'm right."

Finding her voice, she asked, "How could I copy your paintings if they weren't here in the gallery?"

"I brought them in after each trip!" Wesley continued. "You never did one exterior landscape piece until you moved in here and began taking a close look at my canvases."

"Wesley, you're not being rational," Miranda began, still believing she could reason with him. "Can you hear yourself? Do you remember the hike I took you on? My suggestion that you try nature landscapes? That was when you were doing cityscapes exclusively. Good ones."

"Even now, you're still trying to take credit for *my* work!"

Miranda took a breath, then kept her voice as low and steady as she could. "Maybe you should take a look at my résumé in our Co-op brochure. I've been sketching, drawing, and painting naturescapes since I was five years old. You can confirm that with my mother, who's kept every piece of my art from Kindergarten through High School."

Now that the words had started to come, she found she couldn't stop the flow. "I won my elementary school's art prize. I began winning juried wildlife art shows when I was a teenager. I was awarded the highest honor by the art department of my college. And I already have several professional awards, Wesley. I really have no idea what you're talking about."

"That's because you're so mentally myopic, you have no clue what's right in front of you. Your work is derivative, Miranda, and if you can't see that, it just proves my point. Get a career of your own. Get a life of your own."

"A career . . . a life of . . ." she sputtered. "I would be very careful what you say, Wesley, to me or to anyone else. I'm going to report this conversation to my representative, and to the gallery owner. And . . . and . . . ."

"Go ahead! I already have! You'll be hearing from them both!"

"That's ridiculous. And it's a lie." Grabbing the few items she'd planned to take with her, she turned and made a dash for her car, eager to put as much distance as possible between herself and the venomous words her colleague and friend—make that *former* colleague and *former* friend—had spewed at her.

Numb, she couldn't think straight, couldn't navigate toward the park, so she turned back toward her house. Once home, she stared at her studio wall—the one upon which several of her paintings hung—as though seeing her work for the first time.

Now that her heart rate had steadied and she could

breathe again, she asked herself, *Is he right? Have I been copying someone else?*

Then, as she reviewed each image, the thoughts that'd inspired each began to flow, memories so clear they seemed to be embedded in the paint itself. While technique could be, and had been, studied and learned, the source for inspiration had to come organically, and for her, it always had and always would. She would no more use someone else's painting to inspire her own than she would have plagiarized a paper while in college, or a submission, say, to the Duck Stamp competition. The value of anyone's work was its originality. Perhaps it was not her, but Wesley himself, who lacked inspiration and found himself so insecure that he'd chosen to attack her. If she looked closely at his canvases—which she never had—would she find he was, in fact, copying *her*?

Miranda steered clear of the Co-op studio for the rest of the week. She used the time to complete images for a new San Francisco start-up company. She'd met a software engineer named Craig when he came to the studio looking for local artists. His innovative idea was to use e-mail to share local event news with his friends. So far, he hadn't come up with a name, so he just called it Craig's List. Meanwhile, he needed an image.

She offered three simple options: an interlocking set of initials; a 3-bullet-pointed list topped by Craig's signature beret; and the bullet-points next to a silhouette of the Golden Gate. *He may not use any of them. But it's paid work, and I hope he likes them.*

Having added a scanner to her computer desk, since more and more work drafts had to be delivered digitally, she scanned the images, then e-mailed them to Craig. The activity made her chuckle since, after all, his company was based on e-mail.

She also used the week to work through the provenance of her own canvases, asking herself the inspiration source for each piece. Did the image come from her imagination or from a photograph she'd taken? Was the image suggested by a teacher, mentor, or friend, or had it sprung from her own impulse?

She pulled art books from her shelves, sweeping through page after page of the texts to remember when important insights had struck her. She found the exercise tiresome and irritating at first, and then discovered she liked the process and found it valuable.

Having started with a yellow-pad list, by mid-week she headed out to purchase more of her favorite Moleskine journals. She then devoted each pair of facing pages to one work. It started with a tiny sketch or watercolor as an image reference, then she printed the name of the painting. She added journal-style notes about the inspiration, whether a photo, a conversation, a dream, or any source it might've been. By the weekend, she had filled several more notebooks and felt truly uplifted by what she'd discovered about her creative process.

Saturday morning, while Meredith slept in, Miranda

headed out early to make another attempt at the day she'd planned the previous weekend.

She went first to the Co-op Studio, prepared to face Wesley if necessary, but not eager to do so. Happily, he wasn't there. She took her camera out of its bag and began photographing the paintings he'd displayed. Then she took a copy of one of his brochures, which showed other works.

Canvas by canvas, she reviewed his pieces—something she'd never done before, she realized, as she'd only looked at one or two as he'd shown them off to her. *Most of these can be traced to one of my own!* The shock of it left a metallic taste in her mouth. Composition, balance, subject choice—all were derivative of her own work. What he hadn't managed to capture of hers was intensity of focus. But like her, he'd even switched from oils to acrylics.

Perhaps the saddest part of the discovery was that Wesley's earlier work was truly his own. His cityscapes held an energetic focus and came from a distinct vision. Had she somehow pulled him away from his best work? No, she couldn't take the blame. Every artist had mentors and masters whom they admired, who inspired them to ask deeper questions and consider new points of view. The true path of any artist would be impossible to duplicate, as every moment of life's experiences infused the act of creating.

Wesley was actually angry at himself for abandoning

his unique style and for that self-defeating choice there were consequences.

Miranda knew it was time she called her professional rep.

Though Miranda didn't know much about her personal life, she did know Zelda McIntyre to be one of the most successful representatives in the local art scene.

Zelda's tone and manner often reminded Miranda of her mother. Though they hadn't been friends, they were now acquaintances, and to some extent, ran in the same circles.

With offices in both San Francisco and Santa Barbara, Ms. McIntyre was wealthy in her own right, elegant to a fault, and seemed to get her way mostly through a combination of wily negotiation and charm. She could, however, strike terror with a mix of hot demands and icy resolve that Miranda had seen in action only once—and that'd been quite enough.

"Miranda, dear, how are you?"

"Very well, Zelda, thanks. I do have something to tell you."

"Problem?"

"Possibly." Miranda went on to describe Wesley Adams's accusations.

After a long pause, Zelda asked, "Be honest with me, Miranda. Is there any truth to Wesley's claim?"

"None," Miranda snapped back. "And I can prove it."

"Excellent. Avoid contact with him. And leave the rest to me."

Relief flooded through Miranda as she hung up the phone.

Chapter 10

Miranda didn't feel like cooking breakfast on Sunday morning, especially since it seemed unlikely Meredith would be sharing it with her. But when Miranda went to the kitchen to make tea, she was surprised to see her sister already brewing coffee.

"Morning," Meri said in a still-drowsy voice.

"Morning yourself."

"I guess we both slept in. Feel like going out to eat?" Meri asked.

"Sure!" Miranda said. "Have someplace in mind?"

Meredith stirred cream into her coffee while she considered. "Sabella and La Torre," she suggested.

"Fun!"

"Mussels Bordelaise," Meredith said, her eyes lighting up.

"Linguine and Clams," Miranda added, feeling her mouth start to water. "And no need to get fancy."

"Jeans it is." Meredith confirmed, carrying her coffee upstairs.

"Hey, Mer, wanna walk?" Miranda called after her. "It's only fifteen minutes."

'That's the *downhill* time. Back up to the house will take at least twice that."

"True. But we could work off more calories," Miranda pointed out.

"Good argument. I'll be down in ten, with walking shoes."

The two sisters, both sporting hats and long sleeves against the sun, walked straight down Jones Street till they turned right on Jefferson, walked two more blocks and were nearly at land's end. As they approached the Fisherman's Wharf and found the sign for Sabella and La Torre, a blue awning read "If It Swims We Have It." Under it, a line of white holding tanks for fresh seafood echoed the message. They passed under the signature "Entrance" sign and Miranda looked down a row of refrigerated glass cases that presumably offered to-go items. Inside, a host led them to an available leather-benched booth, where the shellacked press board table top held ketchup, hot sauce, sugar packets, and metal-topped glass salt and pepper shakers. At each place setting, a placemat framed a clean, thick white plate, paper napkins, and stainless flatware.

A waiter delivered plastic glasses of water and took their order, promising hot sourdough bread.

"God, I've been working my butt off," Meredith complained, chomping into a slice of fresh bread.

"Same here," Miranda added, sipping water.

Meredith seemed to consider this for a moment, then said, "So . . . pardon my ignorance, but when you say you're working hard, I don't really know what that means."

Confused, Miranda put down her water and looked at her sister.

"I mean, I know you've been painting. You love to paint, have since we were kids. But doesn't that come more under the category of 'fun' than 'work'? Isn't it sort of a hobby?"

Anger shot through Miranda's chest followed by the dull ache of feeling misunderstood. She knew, though, that her sister was simply voicing the majority opinion, and that if she used this as an opportunity, she might be able to clarify something important to her.

"You're right." She swallowed the hurt with another sip of cold water. "Painting *is* fun for me, and always has been. And it's more than that, too. It's necessary. Unavoidable. It's like—"

"Like a puzzle you have to solve?" Meredith offered.

"Sometimes, yes. Exactly."

"Like figuring out that mural in your bedroom. You saw the whole jigsaw in your head, then you painted it."

Joy mingled with relief surged through Miranda. "Yes! And . . . had I seen it but *not* painted it, the thought would always be incomplete. It'd plague me, never leave me alone. I'd dream about it, I'd get distracted by it."

"That's how it is for me when I see a deal for a client. I mean, there it is, the perfect buy, the perfect timing."

"And if the client doesn't agree?"

"Well, I mean, the numbers don't lie. Why wouldn't they agree?" Meredith countered.

"You say numbers don't lie, but aren't they open to interpretation?" Miranda asked.

"Oh, are they ever. I guess I see your point. But speaking of numbers, how do you rationalize doing all this work that you like, but not getting paid for it?"

Now we're getting to the crux of the matter, Miranda thought.

Miranda glanced up at the waiter whose hands were filled with two heavy plates of food, but he walked past toward another table. "I suppose that question is as old as Leonardo and the Medicis. Or older."

"Meaning that artists are supposed to have sponsors?"

"It just means there are those who *do* art, and those who *need* art," Miranda said.

"Really? Need?"

"I know, I know, in our culture art is put over there in the 'optional' category, far away from food-water-shelter. But can the human spirit be whole without beauty and self-expression?"

Philosophical ruminations were suspended when their food arrived, aromas swirling, succulent seafood swimming in sauces.

"Heaven," Meredith said, slurping at the mussels.

"Ditto," Miranda echoed, twirling another fork full of *al dente* pasta.

"I suppose you do get paid occasionally for one of

your paintings, at which point you try to catch up with your bills," Meredith declared.

"Is this you asking? Or is this actually Dad demanding an answer?" *And here we are, two sisters, talking about family matters in a family restaurant, established in 1927 by a man and his son, a restaurant still run by family members.* Miranda shook her head. "Yes, something like that. And I fill in with the commercial work."

"What commercial work? What is that, anyway?"

"It's work for hire. Someone needs an image, a logo, a website banner, a painting for a lobby. Zelda usually finds these for me, but I find some on my own. Or they find me." Miranda sopped up sauce with another piece of bread.

Her sister seemed surprised and impressed. "I had no idea," she commented, her tone sheepish.

The two ate in silence for a few minutes. Then Meredith changed the subject. "What should we take to Mom for Easter? Flowers? I can pick up some potted hydrangeas."

"Perfect. And I'll color some eggs."

"She *loves* the way way you dye your eggs."

"It'll be fun, staying in our old rooms, having an evening and a day with them," Miranda said, hearing a wistful tone in her own voice.

"Ever thought what it'll be like when we don't have them?"

Miranda put down her fork and took a sip of water. "No. And . . . yes."

"Sometimes I kid myself that I'm prepared. But I know I'm not. The financials, all that stuff, is in order. I helped them with their Living Wills, the trust, all that."

"Of course you did," Miranda said, hurt that no one had thought to include her in those significant conversations.

"But that's the least of it, in a way," Meredith continued.

Taking a sip of water, Miranda added, "Best thing we can do is enjoy them while we can."

"Exactly," Meredith confirmed. "Actually, Mother has been helpful about my asshole-at-work problem."

"You're having dificulty at work?" Miranda asked.

"Don't sound so surprised, Mandy. We all have our troubles." Meredith went on to describe Albert's reprehensible behavior.

Then, following her lead, Miranda shared her dilemma about Wesley Adams's accusations.

"Sorry you're having to deal with an asshole, too." Meredith pushed her plate away. "Also, sorry I've been the asshole at home lately."

Miranda choked.

"I've been snippy," Meredith continued, "and rude. That, by the way, is a sincere apology."

"Accepted, sis," Miranda said. "In future, if we make plans, can we communicate when they change?"

"Absolutely," Meredith agreed.

When the bill came, they each put down a twenty-dollar bill. Leaving the change for their waiter, they set off for home, huffing and puffing their way up the long hill to their house. Meredith paused for a moment before heading upstairs. "You know," she said, "you should continue that Bay Bridge mural here to the main floor."

"Really?" Miranda smiled, shaking her head. "That might be the nicest thing you've said to me in recent memory."

"Who knows, maybe my sister's work will be famous one day. Your murals could add to the value of the house. Just keeping an eye on my investment."

Chapter 11

Zelda McIntyre flipped open her Filofax planner for Wednesday, April 12, inserted a special project page, and began making her list.

She'd already done some homework about Wesley Adams, discovering that yes, he did have a rep, and, yes, he had entered a juried show that carried some prestige for landscape artists.

Yesterday, she'd made her first call: to the art show director, asking whether or not he'd heard about Wesley's bonafides being questioned. Using carefully modulated tones, she made the call sound as though she, herself, were more shocked than anyone else about the possibility Mr. Adams might've been copying another artist's work. Hearing the dismay in the man's voice, she felt certain just enough seeds of doubt had been planted for the rumor-weeds to begin winding their way through the artistic community.

Today, Zelda began her list with a series of key phone calls.

The one to Bays Arts would be most urgent, and

after thinking about her approach, she picked up the phone.

The Co-op's "director" was more of an absentee landlord than a true manager. "You realize you've opened yourself up to public censure," Zelda warned. "Not only has my client's reputation been impugned, I'm not entirely sure she's even safe in your facility."

Alarmed, the woman had demanded an explanation, and Zelda was happy to comply, using words like "unstable" and "irrational," as well as "medication" and "supervision." The director tried once more to duck her responsibility by mentioning that "artists are on their own," but Zelda, having pulled the contract before making the call, reframed the burden of responsibility using legal language.

"Ms. Jones has enjoyed her time at the Bays Arts Co-operative Studio & Gallery," Zelda said by means of a closing argument, "but she'll have to think carefully whether or not she wants to continue her membership. It will all hinge upon what the Co-op defines as acceptable behavior. Shall a person who throws out both accusations and threats be able to keep his membership? We'll give you a few days to decide."

Zelda hung up, noticing that her hand shook slightly. While she quite enjoyed getting tough in the context of a good negotiation, she avoided ugliness. If it weren't still early in the day, she might pour herself a vodka martini or a white wine, but the calm from alcohol would have to wait.

Pouring a Perrier over ice with a slice of lime, she returned to her desk and began strategizing a press release. Four months earlier, in January 1995, the San Francisco Museum of Modern Art had opened the doors of its new location, doing its best to steal thunder from both the Museum of Contemporary Art in Los Angeles and the L.A. County Museum of Art. Zelda had made sure to attend the San Francisco opening, and had insisted Miranda go too, making sure to introduce her young client to various leaders of the art world.

That'd gotten both her and her client a mention in the press, but it was time to feed the reporters something fresh. The release would mention Miranda's latest award, another one for her wildlife work. Zelda spared no brainspace to memorize the long list of similar names these award programs all used—all but one—but she kept a file she'd review in a moment.

The one award she *did* remember had been given to the Bennington College senior Miranda Jones in 1992, in the "legacy" category of the Congressional Art Competition. Founded by Congresswoman Nancy Pelosi in that year, the competition honored high school students from the San Francisco Unified School District Arts Festival each spring, and their works then displayed for a year in the Capitol. Miranda had mentored young students in her home town, and Ms. Pelosi had been impressed; so had Zelda and many others.

Now, if Zelda played her cards right, she might get a commitment from the Sloan Gallery to include Miranda in their summer show. That could be the lead, but she'd need to follow with more items of interest.

"She's going off to the Carrizo Plain National Monument next week," Zelda bragged to the gallery director on the phone. "She'll come back with gorgeous pieces featuring this year's super bloom. The flowers will still be in the newspapers when her paintings show up on your exhibit walls."

Zelda knew it was rash to make promises about work not yet created, but she also knew Miranda had at least two paintings of yellow blooms that could be used in a pinch.

When Sloan Gallery agreed to include Miranda Jones in their July show, Zelda said her professional thank-yous before hanging up. She hit the space bar on her keyboard and watched as amber letters danced across the black screen. In ten minutes, she drafted the opening PR paragraphs, complete with all the necessary names and details.

She debated the wisdom of mentioning anything about the altercation with Wesley Adams. There was nothing much to the young man's résumé, but every artist had to start somewhere. According to what she'd read, he'd applied his modest talents to painting cityscapes and had some good success, probably because "edgy" was trending in certain quarters. Had he stuck to that and built on his success, Zelda might even have considered approaching him about representation.

Now, however, the insecure fool had made a serious

mistake. She'd looked through Miranda's meticulous notes and realized that, not only was her client correct; she'd inadvertently laid the groundwork for a lawsuit.

Zelda had every intention of avoiding that, since slander could cut both ways. She knew this from personal experience. Miranda might win the suit; but it would be a hollow victory, leaving mud clinging to what was still a pristine reputation.

Mr. Adams needed to go away, quietly. He ought to return to his home territory painting skyscrapers and brownstones, or do whatever he wished in some other city. But as for getting noticed henceforward in San Francisco, Zelda would enlist the help of others in blocking his advancement. Since he'd been dishonest about copying Miranda's work, sooner or later he would be dishonest about something else as well. No one ever wanted to work with a liar.

Meanwhile, Zelda came up with a slant that would spin the Wesley problem in Miranda's favor. "Possessing a rare mastery of technique in someone so young, the artist has also become known for the integrity of her work because of her tireless devotion to research. Whether camping out for days to observe close-up the spectacular feathers of a rare bird, or placing her own safety at risk by embarking on adventure travel, a Miranda Jones painting has come to be synonymous with authenticity. Since few artists go to such lengths to study their wild subjects, echoes of the artist's work have even been found in the canvases of some of her less adventurous colleagues. Imitation, they say, is the sincerest form of flattery. But why settle for a derivative work, when one can enjoy an authentic Jones?"

Zelda re-read the release, thinking it might be too heavy-handed. Not only that—she'd made it sound as if a Miranda Jones *painting* was camping, rather than the artist. Well, that would have to be corrected. She never sent out releases immediately, but preferred to let them rest for a day, whenever possible. By tomorrow's cold light of day, she might notice a few words that should disappear under her red pen.

Meredith had hoped Thursday would be an easy day so she could daydream about her upcoming Saturday date. Her hopes were foiled, however, when she responded to a request from Ron Mansfield to come to his office.

When she saw his face, a zing of post-traumatic stress ran through her as she feared that, once again, Albert might be sitting behind her boss's desk. It was the senior partner himself, though, who appeared upset.

"Ron? You wanted to see me?"

"Hate to do this to you, Meredith, but I just got a call from Randall Schwartz."

Around the office, the name had come to trigger an in-house version of the old saying. "The bad news is, R.S. called. The good news, it's your turn to handle the call."

"My turn up at bat, I guess," Meredith said, resigned to enduring one of their pesky client's tirades.

"Does a bear go potty in the woods?" Ron said, his smile more like a grimace.

"Was Rome built in a day?" Meredith countered.

"No, and neither was this firm. You know what to do. And I'll say it in advance: thanks."

Meredith uttered a short, mirthless laugh. "You're welcome, I'm sure."

Mr. Schwartz was like a medical patient who thought his own diagnostic skills were more advanced than his physician's. In the portfolio management business, any client had the right to ask questions, and even to second-guess their advisor's choices. Meredith enjoyed discussions with her clients as they reasoned together through a series of choices, gauging risk against security, growth against stagnation, performance against potential.

But Randall's approach was to tear down every bit of work done in the weeks prior to each call, questioning each stock position, but also impugning the depth of work behind each of those choices. So every member of the firm who'd had to deal with him had come away feeling singed, if not actually burned.

And what made this client impossible to dismiss, or ignore, was that he'd actually been a co-founder of the firm, and still owned too big a percentage to be bought out—if he'd ever consent to sell. Ron always promised it would be "worth it in the end" not to make an enemy of Randall. But this was actually a policy of "keep your enemies close."

Meredith returned to her office and placed the call.

"Mr. Schwartz," she began, "Meredith Jones. Always a pleasure."

"I doubt that very much, Ms. Jones. Stuck you with the duty today, did he?"

Meredith debated uttering a denial. Instead she said, "Yes, sir, he did. That which doesn't kill us makes us stronger, right?"

A guffaw echoed through the phone line, and Meredith couldn't help but smile. Ninety minutes later, their trickiest client not only declared the portfolio choices sound; he increased his position in several key stocks.

Before Meredith headed home for the day, she stopped one more time in Ron Mansfield's office. "The vinegar didn't work," she said. "But the honey did."

Ron looked up, his eyes bright in the tanned, still-handsome face despite the wrinkles. "Good for you. That's what I call good client relations."

"Thanks," she said.

"FYI, Albert said not to trust you with the Schwartz account, that he would take it over himself. You just proved him wrong."

Chapter 12

Miranda and Meredith spent Saturday morning doing domestic chores. This being Passover, their favorite deli wasn't available for a bagel run, so they made do with cinnamon raisin toast, scrambled eggs, and a quick kitchen clean-up.

Each of them changed bed linens, dusted and vacuumed their respective floors, took turns doing laundry, and divided the living and dining area tasks. Food would be abundant at their parents' home, so they opted for heating up bowls of soup for lunch, then started the dishwasher.

By 3 p.m. they were each packed and ready to head to Belvedere. Mer had decided she'd drive, and they piled their suitcases into the trunk of her BMW, then placed the lovely bouquet of flowers on the floor behind the driver's seat, surrounding it with beach towels to keep it upright.

They knew the drive as well as the nursery rhymes they'd memorized as children, and the route to their childhood home seemed hypnotic in its ability to evoke memories.

"Does it feel like we're rolling back the clock, heading to Mom and Dad's?" Miranda asked.

"Sort of," Meredith agreed. "Like the work week is sliding away and there won't be anything to worry about except wearing the right clothes and pushing back from the table before we turn into blimps."

Miranda laughed. "I am worried about telling them the Wesley Adams thing. Dad'll likely use it as another excuse to complain about my unproductive career."

"He means well, Mandy. Don't be too hard on him."

"He *is* hard on me. But I'll take it under advisement."

Miranda looked out toward the Marin Headlands as they made their way across the Golden Gate Bridge, and toward Golden Gate Avenue.

Miranda glanced at her watch as her sister's car climbed the steep, curving road that twined up Belvedere Island toward their parents' home, noting they'd made the trip in ninety minutes. She looked down to see large roofs tucked between the tall trees that stood between them, cheek by jowl, offering a crowded version of privacy. Already she could feel the sense of confinement that sparked an impulse to flee. Yet this long, slender peninsula and the two islands connected by causeways offered some of the most desirable real estate in the country, and some of the best views in the world.

Veri opened the front door only seconds after Mer rang the bell, so eager to see her daughters that she gave them a joint hug, barely containing her excitement.

"Right on time!" she enthused. "Your father will be thrilled to see you!"

After offering their mother the elaborate bouquet, which was accepted with suitable exclamations, the girls carried in their bags and left them in the foyer when they heard their father's voice.

"Here they are!" he boomed. "Hugs all 'round!" He hugged Meredith first, then Miranda. "Want help with all that?" he asked.

They both declined, adhering to the unspoken rule that their father was now past the age of being required to do the heavy lifting, at least when it came to luggage.

"We'll be right down, Dad," Mer promised.

Both daughters dutifully carried their belongings upstairs. Miranda stepped into her old room, smiling at the cozy familiarity. Yes, there were the cheerful yellow-checked curtains, coverlet and shams. Mother had added a few new touches. A deeper yellow twill fabric now covered the window seat, and a couple of decorative pillows on the double bed. The mahogany furniture from her grandmother's home gleamed, and the fresh scent of tuberose filled the room from its tall, glass vase.

Miranda hung her Easter outfit in the closet, set the flannel pajamas she'd brought on the bed, and washed her hands in the private bathroom whose white tiles sparkled. Here, too, yellow appeared: hand towels and bath sheets, soaps and a hand lotion dispenser.

Is this where my love of yellow actually began? As an artist, she'd always been a student of color in its many iterations. The most basic, taught in every beginning class, was the color wheel for pigments, based on red, yellow and blue, first developed by Sir Isaac Newton in 1666.

The primary colors—those that couldn't be formed by any combinations of others—were yellow, blue, and red. To arrive at secondary colors, one mixed the primaries, arriving at green, orange and purple. Then came the tertiaries—some of the most interesting—created by mixing a primary with a secondary, giving each new shade a double name, like blue-green, or red-purple.

Architects, interior decorators, clothing designers, wardrobe and make-up experts, color-complexion consultants, all had their theories about analogous and complementary colors.

In addition to the pure study of color itself, there was also the study of color symbolism, which drew from a diversity of cultural references, some of them tribal or religious beliefs from hundreds, or thousands, of years ago. Some ventured into the intuitive-spiritual realm, some of which Miranda found intriguing, at least enough to dip a finger—or a paintbrush.

Yellow was said to symbolize joy. Paradoxically, it also symbolized cowardice or fear, though not so much visually as verbally, in expressions like "yellow-bellied." She also knew from her brief forays into teaching young children that they adored yellow and often used it in their crayon creations.

Perhaps Mother had an instinctive awareness in giv-

ing each daughter a Primary Color room: pale yellow for me, pale red or pink for Meri.

Pink stood for femininity, sweetness, and love of a gentler kind than the passions associated with red. By assigning pink to Meredith, had Mother imprinted her elder daughter with a more traditional connection to all things feminine? Of course, for a first daughter, what parents wouldn't choose pink? Then when the second child was also a girl, they would have to choose something other than blue.

Interestingly, as the two sisters had evolved, Meredith had gravitated to blue, while Miranda loved green. Eventually, it'd been as if each of them owned their colors, and avoided the other so as not to impinge. When Meri bought her sister a garment, it was always green; when Miranda chose a piece of costume jewelry or made a painting for Meri, she always chose blue.

As they grew older, would they reclaim the colors they'd given up? When they no longer lived so close, would they branch into tonalities they'd never imagined?

Miranda stood for a moment longer, looking past the soft yellow-checked curtains at her mullioned windows, down into the garden below, now accented with vivid yellow spires of forsythia. *It's always the first color to come back.* As Earth recovered from winter, at first everything was just brown sticks, except for the forsythia.

Something tugged at the edges of her mind, and she waited for it to come clear, trusting this familiar process. The color . . . it stirred something to life within her.

Primal. Earthy. But electric with newness and freshness. Yellow is a harbinger of something new.

Veri tiptoed down the stairs Easter morning, and opened the fridge to get started on her signature dish for brunch. She let out a little squeal of delight as Pilar unlocked the back door.

"Mrs. V?" Pilar asked, a frown creasing her brow.

"It's Mandy! She brought her colored eggs!"

"Ohhh," Pilar responded, a huge smile erasing her frown. "That's good!"

Veri'd arranged an Easter egg hunt for this afternoon, for some of the neighbors' families. She'd colored some eggs herself and hid them in the back refrigerator, but only an artist like Miranda could create what she called "watercolor-eggs."

Meanwhile, Veri pulled out the carton she'd hard-boiled, but not colored, for use in her Goldenrod recipe. She began to peel the shells, but Pilar quickly took over that job, leaving Veri free to start her Béchamel sauce.

As she stirred flour into bubbling butter, she smiled at the simple joy of having all her family gathered.

Granted, this wasn't a big holiday gathering that would last for days and include several meals and parties. But last night's dinner at their club had been lovely, with friends stopping by the table to chat, giving Veri and Charles ample opportunity to brag and show off their beautiful daughters.

How different they are. Always were. As Charles says, the fox and the lynx. She laughed out loud at that description.

"Miss-es?" Pilar asked.

"Oh, something Mr. Charles said last night, that Meredith is a fox—*una zorra*—and Miranda is a lynx—*una linca.*"

"Oh ho!" Pilar chuckled. "Jes, is true!"

As the two women laughed, Veri had a fleeting thought that she should find suitable stuffed animals for their rooms. *Oh, my word. They're not little girls any more!*

No, they weren't, she reminded herself. In fact, perhaps she should acknowledge the fact by redoing their rooms, so when they did get home for visits they could actually feel like the adults they were. That'd be a lovely project, and long overdue, she had to admit. She made a mental note to ask the girls how they'd feel about it.

Though she knew so few of the details, she sensed their lives were complex. Until Meredith's recent overnight, Veri hadn't realized the ongoing push and pull between the siblings over financial matters. And, of course, it wasn't really about money, but rather about self-worth, and how it was measured, whether internally or externally.

As she added the final, secret ingredient to her sauce—the nutmeg—she promised herself today would be light-hearted and fun, knowing it would be all too brief. Now it was time to begin serving her delicious brunch.

Miranda had awakened in her cheery yellow room and opened her door a crack to gauge how awake the household might be. The aroma of divine cooking smells wafted up the stairs, and she pulled on her robe to hurry downstairs, eager to see what Mother and Pilar were preparing.

"Goldenrod eggs!" she declared. "Perfect!"

"Wouldn't be Easter without them, would it?" her mother agreed.

"Miss Miranda, hot water for tea is ready."

"Thanks, Pilar," Miranda said, finding a tin of loose Earl Grey in the cupboard and scooping some with a brewing spoon. She offered to help with cooking, but both Pilar and Veri waved her off, so Miranda sipped and observed as Pilar toasted the muffins, sautéed the thick-cut maple-cured bacon for the others, and fried some turkey bacon just for her.

Miranda scurried upstairs to shower and change into her sage green linen dress. When she returned, she helped carry platters into the family dining room.

"The pearls look lovely with that dress, Mandy dear," her mother said, passing her en route back to the kitchen to grab the cream pitcher.

"Thanks, Mom. You look stunning, as always," Miranda said over her shoulder. "And you wore yellow!"

"I adore that suit on you, Mother," Meredith said, as they all settled at the table. "Never get rid of it."

"Thank you, Meri dear. I shan't."

"I agree," Miranda piped up. "It's the color of spring, and a primary," she enthused, "and for artists, it's—"

"I propose a toast!" her father interrupted, seeming not to notice Miranda had been mid-sentence.

Though coffee was being served with their brunch, Veri had also divided a half-split of champagne among the four. She nodded at her husband, who lifted his glass and cleared his throat.

"Nice to have you girls home for a change," he said, not quite as elegantly as Mother probably wished. "We miss you, you know, your mother and I. Does her a world of good when you visit," he added, a slight warble in his voice.

"Hear, hear," Veri echoed.

They all lifted their flutes. But as they picked up their plates to head for the sideboard, where piping hot food awaited on warmed platters, no one seemed to notice that Miranda hadn't taken a sip of her champagne.

Miranda placed her overnight bag next to her sister's in the foyer and stood there reflecting on the day for a long moment. She smiled, recalling how the dyed eggs she'd brought had been put to good use at the Easter egg hunt for the neighbors' grandchildren. "Maybe we'll have some of those ourselves, one of these days," Mother had said. Had that wistful note in her voice been genuine? Would she or her sister want children one day? *Not now. Not yet. Maybe someday.*

She walked into the den for final goodbyes. Meredith and Veri were busy comparing notes over an issue of *Vogue*. Charles looked a little bit lost, sitting in his reading chair, his newspaper cast aside. Miranda went to him, and sat awkwardly on his footstool.

"So, sounds like you're keeping busy," her father said, as if both daughters' work schedules hadn't been thoroughly discussed during brunch.

"Yes. Plenty of work these days," Miranda confirmed. "You, too," she added, recalling his recitation of board meetings, fund raisers, and golf games.

"That mural of yours. Like to see it some time," he declared.

Miranda looked up. "Really? Meri and I . . . we'll figure out when we could invite you for dinner."

"Splendid. Speak to your mother."

Feeling both dismissed and encouraged, Miranda stood. They all gathered in the foyer for hugs and farewells.

She waved until her parents were out of sight, then settled into her seat and glanced at her sister, who seemed lost in her own thoughts.

Pensive herself, she said, "This might've been the most relaxed visit to our parents' home in recent memory."

"No arguments, no demands, no real interrogations," Meredith agreed.

"As though all of us were on our best behavior," Miranda theorized.

"I don't know why, but there is a sense of comfort there. Just what a home should have," Meredith commented. "So, is it the lovely arrangements of things? The dazzling clean? The aromas? Or is it just the familiarity?"

"Mother has a knack for turning a house into a home," Miranda offered. "I hope I've inherited enough of her genes that, someday, a family of my own will feel the same."

Chapter 13

Miranda left home early, grateful when her parking strategy worked, and she snagged one of the few spots near Fort Point at the south end of the Bridge. The Fort Point National Historic Site was part of the much larger Golden Gate National Recreation Area, which encompassed the Presidio, Marin Headlands, Stinson Beach, Muir Woods, and even Alcatraz Island.

She grabbed only her camera and began walking. When she came to the trailer that'd become the semi-permanent home of the Welcome Center, she stepped inside to read a brochure. The park had been established in 1972 by a coalition of sixty environmental groups, all of whom were concerned and outraged over plans for huge developments already in the planning stages.

In a city full of historic landmarks, this one, rescued from dense rows of apartments and maintained in its natural state, seemed most intriguing.

This gateway to the Pacific region also had a rich history of guardianship. Fort Point—a military architecture balustrade of masonry topped by one of the smallest of all lighthouses—had been built between 1853 and 1861, during the height of the Gold Rush, by the U.S. Army Engineers as part of a defense system designed to protect San Francisco Bay. The multi-tiered arched brick casemate was enclosed in seven-foot thick walls—the only one of its type built on the West Coast—and was considered the key to the entire Pacific Coast from a military point of view.

During the Civil War, the Army mounted 55 guns. Though the Fort never had to fire during that conflict, it did act as a deterrent. Miranda tried to imagine the fear, and the horrors of a war that tore at the country from within, reaching even to the western edge of the nation.

There were so many more chapters: fortifications during World War II, when the possibility of an enemy submarine stealthily entering the Bay had been a plausible threat. But Miranda shifted her attention to the flora of the park, her eye drawn again by the abundance of yellow blooms.

Grasslands were usually the first to show color, with forbs—plants that were not grasses—flowering early. Though she couldn't name all the wildflowers, she did recognize goldfields carpeting the ridges, noticed poppies waving tiny orange flags, and inhaled the fresh scent of blue blossom.

After snapping several pictures of the colorful array, she searched for a view that would include the Fort Point lighthouse and some portion of the great bridge. She clicked her shutter at the sheer magnificence of the structure—the distinctive orange color and the water below, its gyrations seeming to happen in slow motion. But from this perspective, her lens couldn't capture the lighthouse at the same time.

After several more attempts, she had it: tiny white lighthouse in the lower left, orange sub-bridge arching over it, and the full width of the first tower. She could crop the image to eliminate most of the super-structure, aiming just high enough to incorporate a Marin Headlands mound.

Grinning from ear to ear, she hurried back to her car, eager to begin work on the mural that'd already started to take shape in her mind.

Miranda stood in her bedroom staring at the wall on which she'd just sketched the image she would start to paint later.

She'd dropped off her film on the way home, ordering fast service so she'd be able to pick up her developed prints later. But meanwhile, with the image still fresh in her mind, she'd used black chalk to outline the major elements of her design.

Several days earlier, she'd done homework in the library, and she knew bridges had three main sections: foundation, substructure, and super-structure. Though she could take artistic license in her own murals, she preferred to make them as realistic as possible, which meant she had to know something about proportion to create the right spacing between parts. She believed that the more she understood about the transfer of weight and tension, the more these qualities would intuitively transfer to her images.

Beginning at the lower left corner, she'd outlined the southern abutment of the bridge, the foundational element designed to endure intense pressure. That also aligned with the location within her own building.

Next, she planned to capture the "bridge within a bridge"—the graceful steel arch that'd been specially designed to preserve the historic Fort Point, and now carried the roadway to the bridge's southern anchorage.

The arch would take up about two-fifths of her image, with the remaining three-fifths devoted to the span ending at the first tower. Though the actual distance between the two was 345 meters, that would appear foreshortened from the vantage point she'd photographed, making it part artistic license, part true perspective. She realized that, once again, she'd have to "imagineer" the view to perfectly include both the lighthouse and the bottom of the bridge. But that called for her to see through the buildings that actually stood between her and Fort Point.

How much of the hillside would she include? She loved the idea of more nature than a pure city view. If she painted in an edge of wildflower, her room would live in a perpetual spring, even on cold, foggy days. *And I could get some accent pillows to match the flowers.*

With nothing further to do until her film was ready,

she went upstairs to make herself a cup of tea. She looked out the livingroom window and sipped the hot brew. Murals had never before been a focus, but she greatly enjoyed the process—this new endeavor of "seeing through walls," or seeing what *should* be there.

During their many travels, her parents had met and befriended Gerard D'A. Henderson, a world-renowned artist famous for sculptures, paintings, and murals installed from Hong Kong to Barcelona and many points in between.

One of his most celebrated accomplishments was an 80-foot mural covering the foyer walls of the Sky Club atop the Pan Am Building. The airline's founder, Juan Trippe, while traveling through Asia, had stayed at the famed Mandarin Hotel and admired its murals of Chinese horsemen. A meeting was arranged and, true to form, Gerard began painting on the floor of his studio, creating original ideas before the very eyes of his would-be sponsor. He accepted a commission to paint the history of clipper ships, a breathtaking work even more impressive than the view from the uppermost floor of the skyscraper.

Miranda left her now-cool tea on the kitchen counter and ran downstairs to find the brochures she'd saved about his work. She found one of his quotations: "In my own work as a muralist, I always try to bring in some fantasy, drama and spectacle to delight the public's eye and at the same time remind them of their past cultures and art heritages."

As if a valued mentor had suddenly appeared in her studio, she could hear his voice. A charge zinged through her. *Certainty. Encouragement. Guidance.* Yes. He was telling her she was on track.

One of America's most iconic bridges—could she paint *its* history? Start with the wide-open mouth of the Bay before any bridge existed, then Fort Point. Construction of the bridge, vintage ships passing through the straight. Then the bridge as it stood today, contemporary ships on the water and a jet overhead.

Would a commission as august as Gerard's ever come her way? With renewed energy, she decided to proceed without bothering to collect her photos. She organized supplies, placed two bare-bulbs in portable light stands, and began painting.

Just before midnight, the drying mural shone in the brightened room, as though the wall had been replaced with a solid sheet of glass offering the view that should always have been there.

Chapter 14

Meredith sat at her desk on Tuesday afternoon, avoiding work by enjoying the view from her California Street office in San Francisco's financial district. She was supposed to be reviewing the SOW—Scope of Work—for her new position as Vice President of client relations. The job, which had shifted her from her previous numbers-intensive tasks, held more promise, more money, and more pressure.

"Meredith Jones," she answered in her usual professional greeting when her private line rang.

"Peter Sylvester."

She didn't recognize the name, so she continued with, "And how may I help you today, Mr. Sylvester?"

"By dropping the client-speak, for starters."

On guard now, and slightly irritated, she said, "Sorry, who is this?"

"Peter Sylvester? From the Pacific Conference?"

Now Meredith's brain took a wild turn through the scores of people she'd met four months earlier at a huge financial conference at the Moscone Center. So many possibilities popped up that she had no mechanism for sorting them.

"We talked about Maui, remember?"

Heat flooded Meredith's face as though she'd suddenly slipped into a bubbling hot tub—one of the things they'd discussed over drinks at the end of a long conference day.

"My place isn't far from here," he'd said after a steamy kiss in the elevator.

At the last moment, she'd resisted his invitation. It'd been too convenient. She'd wanted to salvage some dignity.

Now she patted a tissue to her upper lip and took a breath. "It took you long enough."

"Sorry about that. Constant travel."

"Must be nice."

"Nicer to be home, actually. Can I make it up to you?"

She chuckled. "Like how?"

"You don't have anything that needs laundering, do you? Something French?"

"Are you kidding me? You want to take me to the French Laundry?"

"I knew you were quick. Pick you up at four Saturday afternoon, so we can enjoy the drive. Bring your appetite."

"Never fear."

Miranda spent Tuesday updating her professional portfolio. The multi-stepped task, not one she usually enjoyed, seemed urgent, because of Wesley's complaint and Zelda's efforts to clear her reputation.

The project extended until by Thursday, she was carefully lighting—both artificially, and by gauging the appropriate degree of sunlight coming in through the one window—and photographing the new mural in her home studio. She had moved aside her desk, clearing everything on its surface, and given the floor a quick polish. With the room gleaming, the mural took on a special luminescence she knew would show in the finished photographs.

She made a run to her local camera store to drop off her film, driving her car instead of her bike, so she could stop to pick up her sister's dry cleaning and a few grocery items for Meredith, since she herself would be away for a few days as of Sunday.

By Friday night, she felt entitled to put her feet up and watch TV. But a restlessness she couldn't identify made mindless relaxation impossible. Instead, she warmed up a spinach and feta pizza. While she ate at the kitchen table, she reviewed her list of juried shows, recent pieces, and awards Zelda had requested. *But there's something trying to emerge.* She was always more excited about the new paintings she could already start to see in her mind, than works she'd already completed. She knew, though, something lurked at the edge of her awareness—like a planet that would come into view over the horizon.

Meredith, having worked hard the rest of the week, devoted her entire Saturday to preparing for her date. She zipped out to her favorite nail salon first, getting a pedi and a mani with French tips, unable to resist the play on words. When she got home, she washed her hair and prepared her bedroom, just in case they returned here after dinner. She put out some fragrant candles, arranged cushions, lowered the blinds—nothing fancy. Next she considered her wardrobe.

What does he drive? Bet it'll be a sports car. A convertible?

A scarf would be smart, and put her in mind of an outfit her stylish grandmother might've worn in the 1940s—pencil skirt, cashmere sweater-set, and a beautiful silk scarf. *Everything old is new again.* Pencil skirts were back in style, even if they had to compete with the Grunge movement that was now, thank goodness, waning. And silk scarves would never go out of fashion.

A conservative outfit that'll show off my shape. I might have trouble getting in and out of his car. But that just means I can show some leg. Feeling devious—and sexy— Meredith assembled her pieces and laid them across her bed. Teal sweaters would set off her eyes and coordinate well with the soft gray wool of the skirt. It'd be chilly. In lieu of a scarf, her charcoal wool shawl would provide some drama. She could give her date a "reveal" when she let him unwrap her.

"Be still my heart," she said, fanning her face. This might not be true love. But she'd be very happy to indulge in some true flirting, especially since it came with the promise of hot sex.

Miranda called up the stairs. "Mer?"

"Come on up!" Meredith yelled down to her.

Miranda arrived just as Mer pulled on seamed stockings and attached them to a garter belt. Miranda's eyebrows shot up. "Wow. Hot date?"

"I hope so," Mer said with a wicked grin.

"Whoever he is, he doesn't stand a chance."

They laughed.

"Listen, I'm gonna take a drive tomorrow."

"Research for your next painting?"

"Sort of. I . . . I'm feeling restless. Need to get out of the city."

"Where are you headed?" Meredith asked.

"I don't quite know."

Meredith stopped working on her make-up and looked at her sister's reflection in the mirror. "Are you being mysterious on purpose? Or should I be worried?"

Miranda laughed. "Worried? No! I need the countryside. And there's a super-bloom in the Carrizo Plain."

"A what?"

"You know, incredible flowers, mostly yellow. Wild mustard . . . others, too."

"You're not driving all over the middle of California to look at some flowers, are you? I thought you just did that at Golden Gate."

"I did. It's. . . ."

"Oh," her sister continued, "I get it. You've got a secret beau. Fine! You don't have to tell me."

Miranda stood there, uncertain how to reply without getting defensive. She did her best to suppress disappointment and irritation. "It's a work trip, Mer. I'm packing painting supplies, my camera, sketch pads. I'll probably be gone two or three days. Maybe four."

Meredith continued with her makeup. "Have fun! But call me mid-week. I don't want the folks freaking out."

"If I can. I guess I'll see you later . . . or not," Miranda said.

"Who knows? We'll likely end up at his place."

"Well, have a good time."

"I plan on it."

Chapter 15

Meredith hated the idea of staining the beautiful linen napkins with which the restaurant would certainly adorn their tables. Fortunately, Mother had recently discovered and recommended the new Revlon product ColorStay. Meredith had purchased it in ten colors. She brushed on Everlasting Rum, a glossy plum shade. Then she spritzed on Angel Lily, one of her signature fragrances.

When the doorbell chimed, she grabbed her soft gray leather folded clutch, pulled on the wooly wrap, and dashed to open the front door.

"Good. Looks like you'll stay warm," Peter said.

That wasn't quite the response she was looking for, but the sparkle in his eyes seemed promising. Locking the door, she followed him to the curb, where a silver Porsche crouched.

"911 Turbo Convertible," she pronounced.

"Coil and wishbone suspension inclusive," he confirmed.

"And all six gears. Can I drive?"

"I don't know. Can you?"

"Oh, yes."

He grinned. "Maybe next time." He opened the passenger door.

"Fair enough." She took his offered hand to lower herself into the seat, showing just enough leg and garter to make him blink.

She smiled as he rounded the car. He climbed in and asked, "Seatbelt fastened?"

She beamed a smile. "Yes, Sir, Captain."

Meredith found herself rolling over the countryside, alternating between delightful relaxation easing through her limbs and delicious tension tugging at her solar plexus.

Leaving the city behind, Peter drove into the dreamy, idyllic landscape. In the distance, hazy hills formed a patchwork background, the geometric rows of vines highlighted with peachy late-afternoon sunlight.

"We're on a 'hilly pilly' road!"

Peter glanced at her quizzically.

"A childhood memory. What my sister and I used to call country roads like this." As Meredith looked more intently at the vines, she saw that between the rows stood tall stalks fuzzed with tiny yellow blooms. *Maybe that's the wild mustard Mandy talked about. I guess she'd love this.*

"My childhood back seat memories are all about

fighting with my brother over who got to choose the movie. We had this tiny TV with a VHS player Mom used to plug into the cigarette lighter outlet."

They laughed, sharing more small talk about sibling rivalries and family dynamics. An hour later, the Porsche tires crunched over gravel as they approached the long, two-story building with river rock clad walls below, timbers above. Flowering vines climbed pillars along a portico that led into a warren of lovely spaces reminiscent of a French country estate surrounded by gardens.

The host asked whether Meredith would like to keep her shawl. She said "yes," waited till she had Peter's eye, then unwrapped herself, delighted as he indulged in a ravenous gaze that lingered on her sleek legs as she crossed them in his direction, opening the slit in her slender skirt.

"I read about this place," she commented. "It was in the *Chronicle* last year."

"Right. When the Yountville town mayor sold it to Thomas Keller. One of the best chefs in the country," Peter enthused.

"I remember," Meredith agreed. "This isn't your first time here, is it?"

Her question caused a blush to overtake his neck and cheeks. "No," he confirmed. "Not my first. Nor my last, I hope."

I don't mind that the man has a past, Meredith thought. *So long as it doesn't follow him around.*

A waiter offered welcome, explanations, wine list,

and the recitation of the day's two tasting menus. Since the restaurant required pre-ordering, Peter had chosen one of each to give them both the maximum opportunity for sampling.

The chef's signature introductory bite: salmon tartare swirled into the top of tiny *crème-fraîche*–filled cornets, as playful as miniature ice-cream cones, only savory, tangy. Then, small tasting plates: oysters and caviar, lobster and quail, poached peaches and spinach fresh from the nearby organic farms, Bodega Bay crab and Sacramento Delta green asparagus. They passed small plates back and forth across the table.

Meredith began to hear herself oohing and aahing at every bite. "I've never experienced anything like this meal, not even with my family during our trip to the Loire Valley."

Peter grinned, but mostly appeared content to concentrate on enjoying his food.

Meredith, however, couldn't seem to keep her thoughts to herself. "You're not saying much," she said between exquisite bites. "I half expected you to go on about yourself: the money you earn; the trips you take; the victorious battles at work; the irritations of flying First Class; rising property prices in the Bay Area."

"Why?" he asked. "So I could bore you with my self-absorption?"

She laughed. "Well, unlike someone at work who shall remain nameless, you don't seem eager to lord your superior earning power over me."

He touched his napkin to his mouth, then said, "I'm sorry any work-jerk would try to do that. In our business, income can be as volatile as the Dow Jones." His eyes focused on hers. "Other things are a lot more important."

Something luscious coiled through her innards, and this time it wasn't the glorious food. The attraction pulled at her. Was it the thick black hair, the dancing deep blue eyes, the wide shoulders, the long, muscled limbs? *Oh, yes, all good*, she confirmed, taking a moment to savor not only the current bite, but the private view of her table companion.

"I'm glad it's mutual," he said.

His audacious response sent a tingle through her. "Yes," she confirmed. "But I'm enjoying your company, too. This is real fun."

Peter had been careful to drink only one glass of wine. She appreciated that he made a point of it, since he was driving. Summoning wisdom, Meredith followed his lead, and enjoyed a cappuccino semifreddo with the most delectable series of tiny desserts she'd ever tasted: a chocolate confection topped with a delicate candy ribbon bow, donut holes, and a blood orange soda sorbet. The final offering was a box of truffles, from which they each chose one, hers being the salted caramel.

Meredith excused herself to use the ladies' room. As she washed her hands and freshened her lipstick, she thought about the evening. If they knew one another better; if this were, say, a year from now and they were celebrating a first anniversary of a first date, they'd surely enjoy staying the weekend in this gloriously hedonistic setting. She knew there were spas, wine tastings, and other delights to be enjoyed locally. This, however, was that first date with all the attendant anticipation building almost to a fever.

Meredith fanned herself, then walked to the valet station.

"That was sensational, Peter," she sighed while they waited for his car. "I couldn't have imagined it. It was . . . absolutely over the top. Thank you."

A huge smile split his face. "My pleasure," he said, "and I really mean, my pleasure."

Peter put the top up for their drive home, and they rumbled away in the intimacy of the car. She reached past the stick shift and put her hand gently on his thigh. Peter returned the gesture, stroking her knee, then finding the top of her stocking and the garter. "Talk about over the top," he laughed.

By the time they arrived back at her house, neither Meredith nor Peter spared any time for small talk.

They were up the stairs in seconds, half-naked in minutes, with barely a chance for Meredith to show off her satin thong and pushup bra.

He flung back comforter, covers and sheet, scattering the assortment of pillows to the floor.

"Come here," he commanded.

She obeyed, sliding her arms up and around his neck as he lifted her. They toppled, and he sank into her without prelude, moans mingling with orgasmic energy.

"Jesus. Sorry," he managed, when he stopped panting.

"For what?" she murmured. "Just let me know when you're ready to go again."

He did.

Chapter 16

Miranda woke on Sunday morning eager to get an early start. She didn't know her exact route, which made the upcoming adventure even more enticing. She did have one specific goal to see for herself this year's super bloom. And that meant she'd be driving south.

She'd already packed an overnight case, imagining she might stay a few nights along the route. A California map always stayed in her glove compartment, so she'd be able to navigate. In her studio mini-fridge, cut carrots, celery, and some cubed cheese snacks were ready to pop into a small cooler. She did want to take a travel mug of hot tea, though, so before showering and still wearing her skimpy nightie, she decided to run upstairs and put the kettle on.

"I thought you were still asleep," a male voice said.

Startled, she spun around to find a man also spinning in her direction, stark naked.

Her eyes widened while the man grabbed the nearest kitchen towel to cover his important parts.

"Sorry!"

"Sorry!"

"I thought—" Miranda fled back down the stairs.

More or less recovered after a quick shower, she decided she'd prefer to stop at some local café for a hot tea than to brave the upper floor of her house again.

She piled her belongings by the interior door to their garage, then loaded everything into her car. Then hit the external garage door remote to back out of the driveway.

The last thing she heard before closing the door into the house was laughter rolling down from the third floor, and possibly some other sounds she really didn't want to hear.

Miranda beat the Sunday afternoon traffic heading out of San Francisco, berating herself for not having left the day before—Earth Day. Not only would that have been a synergistically perfect day to escape the city for the landscape she craved; she also could've avoided that embarrassing scene in her kitchen.

Water under the bridge, she thought as she glanced left to see the Bay Bridge arching away toward Oakland. Mercifully, the 101, so often choked with traffic, was clear enough this morning that she sped along, avoiding the fork at the 280, and skirting the edge of the San Francisco International Airport.

It took only an hour to reach the southern end of the Bay, where she passed signs for NASA Ames Research

Center. *What incredible minds must be at work on that campus*, she mused. *Maybe I could visit sometime, do some space paintings for NASA.*

Half an hour later, she inhaled the signature fragrance of Gilroy, the Garlic Capital of the World, as their sign proclaimed. If their festival included booths for selling art, she'd consider signing up for a table. But their focus was food, and there were plenty of other places for her to exhibit.

Miranda walked her fingers across the large cassette carry case that sat on her passenger seat, knowing the alphabetically arranged tapes well enough to grab what she wanted with only a glance. Picking up the Pat Metheny's *Secret Story* that'd been released three years earlier, she pushed it into her player and let his lyrical guitar music evoke an emotional response—not just feelings, but memories, insights, and connections she either hadn't made or had forgotten.

"Always and Forever," the wistful melody set against romantic strings, brought up a sadness she'd been suppressing.

What did she want to get away from? Meredith, was one answer. Much as she adored her sister—and she did—she knew they were cramping one another's style. Mer had a unique way of going at life, of testing things to see what worked, whether in the workplace or in the bedroom. When something didn't fit, she let it go with an ease Miranda could only envy, as that kind of detachment eluded her.

Miranda approached things with more caution, but also with more intuition. And intuition figured in the calculus of this free-form drive. Having admitted she was using the time to *get away*, she also had to admit she wanted to *get to* . . . somewhere. But where?

Two hours passed while she listened, mused, and continued south on the 101 until, seeing the sign for Paso Robles, she decided to stop for lunch. She headed east on the regional highway 46, then found the large, grassy square in the town's center. She'd investigate some of the galleries and find out more about the plein air painters groups in the region.

After a quick salad at a charming café, she wanted to find information about local events. The Paso Robles City Library, housed in a beautiful historic building, was closed today, and so was the Chamber of Commerce, but next to its closed door she found a bulletin board. Sure enough, there she found information about S.L.O.P.E.— San Luis Outdoor Painters for the Environment. She read the name again with a sense of longing, knowing she lived too far away to join.

Ah! The freedom of the day: no set schedule, and no determined destination. Yet some insight was making its way to the surface, pressing her onward. And, from a practical perspective, she knew that before the sun went down she should figure out where to stay the night.

She retraced her route back to the 101 South, thinking she'd make a decision once she reached San Luis Obispo. But when she saw a sign for the continuation of the 46 West, impulse made her edge her Mustang into the right lane, flip on her signal, and head west.

She drove past vineyards with lovely buildings and flags, and inviting tasting rooms. Some properties were ranches, with cattle grazing and the flash of silver windmill blades.

The rural highway was known as Green Valley Road, echoed by its lush green foliage. Hills shouldered up on either side, bringing closer the shrubs and trees she could not name. Her soul drank in the landscape's ability to cancel the now distant city grime and pollution.

Suddenly the coziness of the mountain pass unfurled, expanding to such a vast openness that she felt she sat in a glider. A large unpaved turnout appeared, and she slowed, crossing the double yellow lines to stop at its farthest edge.

Turning off the car, she grabbed the camera and walked to some boulders. Breathtaking! To the far left, Morro Rock anchored. In the middle, blue Pacific sparkled. And to the right, green and golden hills tumbled.

A soft haze hovered low, softening the horizon till it blended with sky. Yellow blooms raced down the hillsides, bright yarn crocheted into quilts draped over the grasses made brilliant green by the rains of winter and spring.

The clouds parted, shifting the metaphor from fabrics to metals, the hills gilded in gold, with the distant ocean giving off the dull shine of pewter.

Then, as long strands of cotton drifted across the sun,

the quilts reappeared, their patterns defined by rows in vineyards, and dotted with the rectangles of hay bales.

Yellow. My harbinger. It's here.

Miranda turned right when she reached Highway 1, surprising herself by heading north. *True North.* She'd been cycling through her Metheny cassettes, and when Metheny's "The Road to You" began to play, she chuckled.

The first town she came to was Cambria, though little of it was visible through the thick stands of pine on either side of the two-lane highway. She pressed on, moving beyond the pines to a sweeping open view of blue Pacific.

So taken with the open water, she could hardly keep her head from turning left. The west side of the road sloped away to a gorgeous strip of land, partially hidden and so enticing she imagined secret houses and private beaches.

She saw signs for San Simeon and the famous Hearst Castle. It'd been years since her parents had taken the family to explore the sumptuous buildings, the sculptured grounds, all designed by the great Julia Morgan.

But a visit would have to be for another time. Heading south again, she saw a sign for Milford-Haven, familiar, though she didn't know why.

A sign pointed left toward Main Street, and another pointing right indicated "No Services." Knowing the road to the right must lead toward residences, she decided to wander past houses before heading for the commercial district.

To her right, houses sat atop a long, meandering bluff with nothing but ocean for back yards. Some were Maine-inspired clapboard with tiny planter boxes in front; some were modern slices of redwood and glass; a few sprawled across larger pieces of property.

Then the houses came to an end, a long gloriously empty meadow of natural grasses stretched away, and at its southern border a shrouded home perched atop a curving bluff that jutted out into the sea.

Something in the view sent a shock through her system, and she pulled to the right shoulder. "My sketch," she said aloud. "And that little watercolor I did in the Dogpatch Café." She scrambled for her purse and the small sketchbook she always carried. She flipped through pages.

"Oh, my God." She held the small image up against the windshield, marveling at the uncanny similarity between something drawn from her imagination, and the real scene before her.

She peered at the bluff, and at its edge noticed a lighthouse partially obscured by a huge tree. Beyond and somewhat behind it, stood a massive home, sheltered in a grove of cypress. And in the foreground, racing along, were the bright stands of lacy mustard, shining vivid yellow.

Miranda, still stunned, pulled back onto the highway but exited almost immediately, to enter the town of Milford-Haven.

She parked the Mustang on Main Street, got out of the car and stretched. Grabbing her purse, she headed toward a corner restaurant called Sally's, with yellow awnings. *How could I resist?* She stepped into a homey room with booths, tables, a long bar, and chintz curtains at the row of windows.

"Help you?"

A pert blonde stood near the bar, and Miranda thought she detected a Southern note to her speech. "Hot tea?"

"You bet. I'll bring out a selection. Sit anywhere you like."

Miranda chose a small table by a window, and a moment later she thanked her for the small porcelain pot of hot water, the matching mug, and a small basket of tea bags in various flavors.

"Jest visitin'?"

"Yes."

"Well, hope you kin stay a whal, so purdy this time o' year."

"It is! Um, what would be a good place to stay, would you say?"

The woman put a hand on her hip, which she thrust to one side. "Wail, if you like the hills, stay up at the Lodge. But if you like the ocean, stay down on Touchstone Beach. I think the Belhaven's the very nicest one of all."

"The Belhaven," Miranda said, pulling out her sketch book, and writing down the name on a blank page. "Sounds great. Thank you!"

"We'll be closin' soon, now, but we open bright 'n early!"

The waitress walked away. But Miranda, needing to know, called her back to ask, "Are you Sally?"

"The one and only!"

Chapter 17

Meredith could hardly believe it was already Wednesday. At work, things had ramped up in both intensity and velocity: just the way she liked it.

Meanwhile at home, she'd felt more settled and peaceful than she had since moving in. Though she hated to admit it, the only reason she could think of was her sister's absence. Sweet, kind, clever, creative Miranda could also be a distraction, and an obstruction.

Peter hadn't called since their spectacular date. And once again, the only reason she could think of was that moment when he'd run into Miranda. He'd explained that, when he heard someone's footfall, he'd naturally assumed it'd been Meredith. He'd been ready to jump her bones again right there in the kitchen. But, to his chagrin, it'd been another lovely lady.

If anyone had been to blame, it was *herself*, she knew. Still, the moment, which had seemed funny at the time, now stuck in her craw as another irritation she had no idea how to handle. For now, Meredith relished the privacy of having the house to herself. Mandy had left a phone message to say she'd be away for at least another day or two.

Meredith knew she wanted to buy Mandy out, but her sister didn't really have a financial stake in the home. She'd be figuring out arrangements with her parents. Where that would leave Miranda, she didn't know, but it really wasn't her problem. Meredith could drain her savings and do the buyout now, but that wouldn't necessarily be the best use of cash.

She wouldn't mind sharing her space with Peter, but she had no intention of calling *him*, because she enjoyed playing the longer game, which required patience.

Meredith's phone rang, jolting her out of her naked man reverie.

"Meredith Jones," she said in her cool, professional voice.

"Ms. Jones, I understand you give excellent financial advice. Would you be available to meet with me?"

"Perhaps you could tell me a bit more about your financial needs before we meet, and then I'd be happy to," Meredith said.

"Oh, I find telephone conversations about these matters to be impersonal. I'd much rather meet, even if it's only for a coffee. Would this be a convenient time?"

Meredith stayed silent for a long moment, trying to think how to respond to such an unusual request. This woman hadn't been vetted, and Meredith didn't make a habit of meeting total strangers, so as not to waste her time, but also as a matter of safety.

"I could make an exception, but my time is limited. We do have a meeting room here at my firm, and we certainly have refreshments," Meredith offered.

"Excellent, I'll be up shortly."

The woman hung up, and Meredith buzzed her assistant. "What was the name of that last caller?"

"Sylvester," Priscilla answered.

An unpleasant zing scorched Meredith and she took a deep breath. *Odd. But obviously no relation.*

Ten minutes later, Meredith responded to Priscilla's summons and made her way to one of the private meeting rooms, where a gorgeous strawberry blonde stood in Bruno Magli stilettos clutching a Chanel handbag.

Meredith stepped into the room and extended her hand. "Ms. Sylvester? Thank you for stopping by. How may I help you today?"

The woman swung toward Meredith but ignored the outstretched hand. "Help me? One thing I do not need is your advice." The woman drew out the final "S" sound as though hissing. "But here is my advice to you," she continued.

Confused, but wary, Meredith waited.

"Stay. Away. From. My. Husband."

Mrs. Sylvester sashayed out on the pointy high heels. Meredith watched as she pushed the elevator's down button, then sank into one of the chairs to keep from falling over, as the blood rushed out of her head.

Meredith made it through the rest of the morning and worked straight through lunch, seething at her desk.

She'd run through her entire vocabulary of expletives, then made up a few new ones. Next, she'd imagined various kinds of revenge, including the removal of certain tender parts. Now, she needed to smash a few things and burn a few others, to get that cheater out of her mind, her memory, and her phone book.

Her assistant said Ron wanted to see her. Meredith could hardly ignore a summons from the boss, so she told Priscilla she needed five minutes, then would go to the senior partner's office.

She stopped in the women's room to pat cold water on her face, freshen her lipstick, and practice a few facial expressions that didn't include fire darting from eyeballs. Somewhat calmed, she made her way down the corridor to the large corner office.

"Ron, you wanted to see me?"

"Meredith, come in!" he enthused.

She smiled politely, determined to conceal any anger.

"I have some great news."

Before Meredith could inquire, Ron pressed on.

"I don't know what exactly you said to Randall Schwartz the other day."

A fresh worry worming its way through her gut, she could only think that somehow Albert had messed things up after her own conversation with Ron's former partner.

"But you made the man very happy," Ron continued.

Meredith had to school herself to stop imagining and start listening.

"He's put another nice chunk of funds into the business, thanks to you. And we now owe you a nice fat bonus."

Meredith sat still, the bad of the day temporarily canceling out the good. She took a breath. "That's nice," she offered. "What do you mean by nice and fat?"

Ron laughed. "That's why I trust you, Meredith. Always cut right to the bottom line. A hundred large."

Meredith's mouth fell open. "Really?"

"I did say he put in a nice big chunk, didn't I? Congrats. You earned it."

She left her boss's office in a strange state, as though one side of her was burning up, while the other froze. The anger she felt at the personal and intimate betrayal certainly burned like a hot coal at her center. But there was nothing like some cool cash to douse the flame.

Now, at the end of a very long and difficult day, she decided to count the win and kick aside the loss.

If P— . . . that man who shall be forever nameless ever calls me again, I'll have no reaction whatsoever. He's not worth the time, the energy, or the regret.

Chapter 18

Miranda had awakened on Monday morning to the sounds of ocean waves and singing birds. Joy had coursed through her as she'd stretched in the Belhaven room's comfortable bed.

She glanced around at the matched set of carved pine furniture that stood nicely arranged, with a television tucked into an armoire, and a gas fireplace waiting to take off the chill of evening.

She showered quickly and dressed in the dark green jeans and white blouse, pulling on a forest-green sweater. Then she left a voice message for Meredith, saying she'd likely be away another night or two.

When she stepped outside and filled her lungs with the freshest air she'd inhaled in months, she couldn't resist a short walk on the bluff opposite the Belhaven. Then, when her stomach rumbled, she aimed the Mustang for Sally's on Main Street, chuckling to herself again as the song "Mustang Sally" came to mind.

Having enjoyed a fresh bran muffin and a mug of Earl Grey, she stepped to the counter to pay her bill.

"Sleep good?" Sally asked.

"Perfect," Miranda confirmed. "Is it always this peaceful?"

"Oh, ye-yes. The ocean breeze keeps it so much cooler than up top in Paso and Atascadero. And we don't get much bustle here in Milford-Haven, 'cept when the tourists come after Memorial Day."

Miranda sighed. "Lovely town. And I love your place. I bet I'd become a 'regular' if I lived here."

Sally beamed a sunny smile. "Why don't you, then?"

Miranda spent the day exploring, doing reconnaissance about the local galleries, leaving her own brochures where she could. She saw a sign for the Environmental Planning Commission, an organization she'd never heard of. Curious, she stepped inside and met Samantha Hugo, a tall, glamorous woman with a presidential air. Sam—as she asked to be called—might be her Mother's age, equally beautiful in a different way. They chatted about ecological issues and wildlife, evidently favorite topics for both of them.

Tuesday's most exciting event was an invitation to join members of S.L.O.P.E. on the next day's journey to the Carrizo Plain for a day of plein air painting.

Wednesday morning she'd risen especially early to grab a quick bowl of oatmeal at Sally's, which always opened at 6 a.m. Sally wished her a good paint-day, and

Miranda drove to the combination self-service gas station and car wash at the far end of Main Street.

She'd be driving about 80 miles round trip, some of it over unpaved roads. Still, she wanted the car cleared of road debris and her tank full before she met the other painters with whom she'd be caravanning.

When she'd replaced the gas nozzle, she glanced up in time to catch sight of a man who'd just finished wiping his car dry. Though she only saw him in profile, he cut a fine figure: wide shoulders captured in a plaid shirt, tight-fitting jeans over a sculpted lower body, a gorgeous head of dark hair.

He yelled, "See ya, Kevin!" waving at another man. His voice, rich and deep, seemed to pour over her like warmed syrup.

"Take care, Cornelius!" the other man answered, waving back.

So that one is Cornelius. And this one is Kevin. After reading the instructions for dropping coins and operating the water spray gun, she hit the trigger. The hose straightened and shoved her back against her car. She was using both hands to try to control the forceful, dancing snake when Kevin came to her rescue. He reached exceptionally long arms across her to grasp the device, then held it as if it were only a garden hose.

"Thanks!" She looked up . . . and up at him. His expression of patience and kindness made her smile. "How tall are you?" she blurted.

"Six eight," he confessed.

"Sorry. I bet everyone asks you that."

"Right you are. But not everyone needs help roping in a wild hose."

She laughed.

"I'm Kevin."

"I'm Miranda."

"Haven't seen you before. Passing through?"

"Here to paint."

"You mean like . . . houses? I've been known to do that. I work for a construction company."

"Oh, that's great. No. I do art, like landscapes and wildlife."

People called out as they drove by, showing Kevin's obvious popularity. *He must make a habit of helping people.*

He made sure the hose behaved as she finished washing her car. As they worked, she explained her plans for the day.

"Well, I gotta get to work. Hope you have a great time painting today."

"Thanks again," she said, pulling away.

Miranda shielded her eyes against the morning sun, following two other cars up Green Valley Road. The mountain pass shimmered gloriously, but she knew what she'd see today would outshine this lovely scenery along Highway 46. They all turned south on the 101, traveled about 30 miles, then turned west on the 58 toward Santa Margarita.

The group whose goals and practices she so much admired, with their slogan "Painting to Preserve and Protect," used art for awareness and education about the Central Coast, which included open space but also ranches, wildlife, and farmland. Their goal could be called selfish: they always wanted to have something beautiful and natural to paint. But in the process, they built community by collaborating with conservation groups, and they put on exhibits, talks, and even panel discussions about art as "connective tissue" between people and preservation.

Among their favorite activities was setting up easels in meadows and fields, and getting to work while the public watched or asked questions. Miranda felt nervous at the prospect of having people hovering and looking over her shoulder. But she understood herself well enough to know she'd soon lose herself in the painting process.

As they joined a much larger caravan of cars, Miranda paid only as much attention to the road as absolutely necessary, because she found it hard to tear her gaze away from patterns of orange, blue, and, most impressively, yellow.

In the foreground, goldenbush stood thigh-high alongside the road, stretching as far as the eye could see. As the dense array of flowers marched away, perspective seemed to make them coalesce into a solid swath of yellow right up to the edge of the distant range. Then the mountains were draped in tapestries running in various diagonals only the hand of a divine seamstress could craft.

The strange sight of a perfectly white lake rested in the center of the long valley, as though a block of ice were surrounded by colored frosting. Soda Lake, made entirely of glistening white salt, surrounded by a vast grassland and rimmed by high mountains, was the largest natural alkali wetland in Southern California.

Though the national monument lay within SLO County, it was only a hundred air-miles from Los Angeles and was home to the Temblor Mountain Range, which ran parallel to the San Andreas Fault. McKittrick Summit towered in the middle of the range at 4,330 feet.

When Miranda finally squeezed into a parking place, she found the other painters and learned what direction they'd be heading—not in a tight cluster, but pleasantly spaced so everyone could see clearly to work.

She gathered her folding art-table, brush carrier, small water bottle holder, and a supply of Claybords. She popped her wide-brimmed hat on her head, slid into her backpack, locked her car, and headed out into a nearby field.

Finding a spot, she set up her table, which unfolded into two working trays, and an easel. Her colors and brushes arranged, she stood back and did a few Tai Chi movements to get centered, calm, and receptive.

When she looked up, she zeroed in on the tonalities of yellow, coming up with names: goldleaf, French's mustard, ochre, dijon, saffron, butter, cheddar cheese, forsythia, blond, marigold, ginger, corn, honey, butterscotch, dandelion, and pineapple. She laughed. Every one of those shades, and more, blew in the breezes. There were adjacent tonalities, where poppies wove through the goldenbush: apricot, cantaloupe, and tangerine.

Partly, the color variations would be inherent in the individual blooms. In addition, the degree of proximity would be a factor. But nothing played with the colors more than the light dancing between clouds—blazing past dense cumuli one minute, and filtered down to softness by strati the next.

As she stood there, a sense of vastness suddenly swept over her and she inhaled sharply as though stung. *Remember to think big,* a message seemed to whisper on the wind. *Cozy comfort is important at home, but we are a part of the immensity of this universe, less limited than we may believe.*

Astronomers, looking through their telescopes by night, must constantly be struck by this. *How do they keep from being overwhelmed?* She could feel the pull of the sky, the ache of the mountains, the ripple of seismic energy that must travel this plain cleft by the San Andreas.

This was a Maker's valley, a laboratory where God tried out Her new ideas, the studio where She drew giant brushes through primordial paint, and where relentless change swirled until beauty reigned supreme.

Miranda listened to the hum of conversation around the table as though it were music.

Her new colleagues had decided to meet for dinner in San Luis Obispo, inviting her to join.

"The purple bush lupin made a drop shadow behind the linanthus," said a painter named Rosanne. "I couldn't have come up with that composition if I'd tried."

"Linanthus . . . is that the yellow with the orange center?" asked Dennis.

"Right," the first painter confirmed. "Though I sometimes get it confused with the yellow rancheria clover."

"I didn't know a single one of those names before today," Miranda admitted.

"Yeah, it takes practice," said Dennis. "But you'll get it."

Though he might have been referring only to the floral nomenclature, Miranda felt his comment described the entire endeavor. Plein air painting had its own rigors. She usually spent her time in the wild capturing what she saw on film, then returning to her studio to paint. What landed on the canvas were images recalled from moments in the field, assisted by her photographs, which boosted specific memories.

But there was less safety in painting "live," and less stability in the view each artist worked to capture, as light shifted moment to moment, or as animals changed position.

Miranda looked around at the new colleagues, some of whom might become friends. She relished the companionship with these like-minded artists.

Water flowed in the creek alongside their table, situated on a wide deck with umbrella tables. Dining *al fresco* seemed the perfect way to conclude a day of painting *en plein air.* A soothing breeze began to lull her toward rest.

Tired from her long day, and mindful of the forty-minute drive back to her motel in Milford-Haven, she thanked everyone again and walked to her car, holding close a new sense of belonging.

Chapter 19

Miranda glanced once more around her comfortable room at the Belhaven, then climbed into her Mustang.

She'd taken an early walk along Touchstone Beach, run into town for breakfast at Sally's, then spent some time updating her watercolor journal.

A multitude of fresh miniature paintings now nearly filled the brand new journal she'd brought on the trip. And one larger canvas stood carefully braced in her back seat. This place—so new, but so familiar—fed her soul and filled her with expectations, like the song from *West Side Story:* "Something's Coming."

Work waited for her at home, and she didn't have the money for another night at her motel, so she knew she should get on the road soon. But she couldn't resist one more walk down Main Street.

She stopped again at the gas station to fill the tank, and to glance around for that man she'd spotted yesterday, but saw no one familiar. She walked to the Sawyer Construction company office where Kevin had said he worked. She poked her head in, but neither he, nor any-one else, seemed to be at the large desks.

As she continued, she saw Samantha Hugo coming toward her and waving.

"Oh, good, you're still here. I wasn't sure where you were staying."

"Hi. Good to see you again."

"Listen, I know this may seem sudden, but we had a meeting last night."

"We?"

"Oh, sorry, the Town Council. We've been looking for an artist to do a mural for us, and when I saw your bro-chure, I thought you might be a candidate."

Miranda's eyes widened. "I love doing murals! In fact, just lately I—"

"I know," Samantha interrupted, "because I talked to your representative, who says you've just completed two murals in San Francisco. I know it's a lot to ask, but is there any possibility you'd be able to spend enough time in Milford-Haven to do one for us?"

Miranda stood there unable to utter a sound.

"Do you have time for a coffee?" Samantha asked.

"Of course! Tea, though."

A host seated them in Linn's Restaurant, elegantly rustic with a farm goods store in front and tables in back. Once they ordered, Samantha leaned forward.

"I know this is sudden for you, but the Milford-Haven Town Council has been discussing this for months. We want to support the Marine Life Management Act."

"Oh, wow. And a mural would help?"

"We hope so. But I'm getting ahead of myself. The California Legislature is discussing this new Act, which would mean preserving habitat along the coast. But it will also mean restrictions on fishing and on pollution, both of which tend to be unpopular."

"Oh, yes. I'm aware," Miranda said, blowing across the top of the hot tea that'd arrived.

"We have two specific goals that we think a mural would address," Samantha continued, adding cream to her coffee. "One, we have something of an eyesore in the middle of town—an empty, unpaved area, next to a commercial building with a large, blank wall."

"Yes, I've seen it," Miranda said.

"Well, we'd like to beautify that area, in keeping with the well-kept store fronts along the rest of Main Street. Even our local builder-developer agrees with that."

Miranda wondered whether this might be the person Kevin worked for, but didn't want to interrupt.

"So everyone agreed a mural was a good idea. It was harder to get agreement on the subject matter. Some said it should depict the history of the town. Some said it should have fake windows and doors, to fool the eye."

"Right, *trompe-l'oeil*," Miranda agreed. "That's a beautiful style and can work well in the right location."

Samantha sipped coffee before continuing. "Agreed. But why not take this opportunity to create a reminder that we're a coastal community, and that precious sea creatures are our neighbors?"

"I couldn't agree more! I love the idea."

"Oh, I'm relieved. Actually, I'm elated! I've seen some of your work, in case I didn't tell you. I go up to San Francisco sometimes."

Miranda felt her face flush.

"Now, we need to work out logistics, finances, and schedules. Can you walk with me to my office?"

Miranda felt so giddy on her drive home that she drove straight through without stopping.

Zelda and Samantha had discussed the details, and with the ink barely dry on the faxed copy of her brand new commission, images of whales and dolphins, otters and sea lions, fish large and small already swam through her thoughts.

The work would be exciting, a privilege, a challenge. But the *timing* of the commission made her heart race. Was it possible that she'd asked the Universe a question and received an answer so quickly? That's how it seemed to her. Would she be brave enough to accept the answer, and let her life move forward on this rising tide of synchronicity and opportunity?

At the very least, she'd be spending enough time in this new place to have a good look around. They'd offered her a guest cottage for a month, and enough of a fee to make the move possible. And they weren't pressuring her to begin immediately.

Would a move make sense to her parents? No. Would her representative go along with it? Reluctantly. And what about her sister?

All these were concerns of the *head*, she thought, and step by step, she could work them out. But another song began to play in her head: "Are You Going with Me?"

Her fingers danced across the cassettes in the case on her passenger seat and she pulled out Metheny's *Off-ramp*. Oddly, the tape was cued to the start of that very song.

If any music expressed anticipation and a journey undertaken, this was it. The gentle, persistent rhythm of bass, drums and chords chugged along like the steady thrum of wheels on a railroad track. But floating above, like an eagle keeping pace with the train, the lyricism of Lyle Maze's electronic piano rode the updrafts and offered a view from higher overhead.

The open highway lay ahead in golden afternoon light. Miranda turned up the volume and opened her window. Air raced into the car and lifted her long hair, which seemed to ride the wind the same way Metheny's high, ethereal guitar solo rode the rhythm track, until the closing strains resonated like whale song in her ears.

Meredith spent Thursday working hard, thinking carefully about managing her new bonus, and ruminating over the visit from Mrs. Sylvester.

In mid-afternoon, she'd asked Ron's assistant for a brief end-of-the-day meeting, and now she took the chair across the desk from her boss.

"There she is, my favorite VP of Client Relations," he welcomed.

Meredith couldn't help but laugh. "Ron, I'm your only VP of Client Relations."

"I don't give myself enough credit for being smart about whom I hire and whom I promote."

She blushed, delighted with the praise, but also mindful of what she'd come here to tell him.

"I don't suppose you're here to give back that bonus, are you? Or to tell me you already spent it all?"

This time, she couldn't summon the laugh he probably expected.

He glanced at his watch, then slid open his bottom desk drawer and drew out a bottle, wagging his eyebrows. "End of the work day. Care for a splash?"

She began to demur, as she usually did, but changed her mind and nodded yes.

"Uh-oh. You never accept my offered libations. Something *is* on your mind."

"Afraid so."

Ron stood up, closed his door, then poured two fingers of Scotch into each of two glasses he pulled from a cabinet below his credenza. Offering her one of the drinks, he said, "You'll solve it, whatever it is."

She sighed, took a sip, and waited while he settled in his chair and swirled the amber liquid in the bottom of his glass. "Do I need to call the lawyer, the doctor, or the undertaker?"

Meredith choked, shaking her head. Then she inhaled and said, "I had a fling with an inappropriate person."

Ron sipped at his drink. After a long pause, he asked, "And you're telling me this because?"

"Because the person tracked me down, came to the office."

He flashed her a look of concern for the first time. "The *person*?"

"The wife. The wife I didn't know about."

Understanding dawned in Ron's face, and Meredith felt herself blush.

"This been going on for a while?" he asked.

"No," she said, with more emphasis than she'd intended. "One date."

"One?"

"One too many."

Ron's face darkened. "You don't mean he . . . He didn't—"

"No! No, nothing like that. He seemed . . . I thought . . ."

"You don't need to explain, Meredith. How can I help?"

Meredith looked at this man who was both friend and mentor, in addition to employer. "I don't need help with anything, Ron, and it's over. But because his wife came here, pretending to be a prospective client, and I met with her in the conference room, I just . . . I wanted you to know. I don't see how she could construe . . ."

"I get the picture. She's aggressive, accusatory. I'll need both their names. I want to get some basic info on both of them, keep the data on file. I'll notify legal."

"Oh! I wouldn't want to bring any sort of—"

"No, I understand. And we won't bring any action at this point, either. But here's the thing. If she was expert enough to find you and deliver her threat, whatever it was, she's likely done this before. Are they a team of extortionists? We don't know. Does he know the wife stalked you? We don't know that either. But here are two things for you to know. First, we protect our own, and we have your back."

Meredith gulped the lump that'd formed in her throat.

"Second, you get points for coming to me. I might never have found out, but you never know."

"No, you never do," she agreed.

"And you can't be too careful."

"God, if only I had been!"

Ron paused, then said, "We all make mistakes, Meredith. I've made my share, and don't ask, because I won't tell. The thing is to learn from them."

"Right. I was a total idiot. I can't believe I didn't see it coming."

"Next time, you will."

Meredith put down the partially finished drink and stood, trying to formulate some suitable way of thanking him.

"Nothing else needs to be said. We don't need to talk about this again, unless we do."

Meredith pressed her lips together and nodded.

"Just don't embezzle from the special client fund, okay?"

She felt her eyes fly wide open in horror.

"Kidding! Meredith, that was a joke. Now get out of here and go home, and find another kind of cure for the lonelies, okay?"

"Yes, sir." It was all she could think to say.

She closed the door behind her quietly, then walked back to her office to collect her purse and briefcase. And she walked more easily than she had en route to see Ron. Now there was no secret, and she could feel the toxicity begin to drain away.

The support of her mentor meant everything to her. She wouldn't let him down again. Nor would she ever let *herself* down.

Fool me once, shame on you. She now had the first part of the old adage well-learned. She'd make sure the second part never had to be learned the hard way.

Chapter 20

Miranda pulled into the garage of the home she shared with Meredith, feeling as though it no longer belonged to her.

She'd only been away a few days. But everything had changed.

She pulled her suitcase and all the other travel items from her car and carried them across the lower-level threshold.

She walked into her studio, smiling at first sight of the Bay Bridge mural, and pausing for a moment, imagining the new mural she'd soon be painting in Milford-Haven.

As though a gleaming shadow swam through the painted water on her wall, she imagined a great whale passing under the bridge, and heard the deep rumble of his echolocation signal.

"I'll be there soon," she said out loud.

She stepped into her bedroom next, smiling again at the bright yellow blooms that strafed across the wall, as though she'd brought the flowers home from her travels. For at least another few weeks, she'd enjoy these rooms that now seemed to have been staging areas for the next chapter of her life.

Miranda climbed the stairs to the kitchen, and when she saw a plastic-wrapped package of ramen on the counter and water just coming to boil on the stove, knew her sister was home.

Sure enough, Meredith came down from her bedroom wearing comfortable sweats and glasses pushed up on her head.

"Hey, Kiddo," she said, embracing her sister.

"Hey yourself."

"Well, you seem . . . different. Like you let a lot of wind blow through your hair and air out your brain."

Miranda laughed. "That about covers it!" She paused. "Are you okay?"

"Yup!" Meredith said, a little too forcefully. "Want soup?"

"Sounds good."

The siblings got out placemats and chopsticks, then settled at their wide kitchen island.

"So," Meredith said, blowing across the steaming noodles she held aloft over her bowl. "Tell me everything."

"There's so much, Mer," Miranda said. "New opportunities. New perspectives. New . . . just new."

Meredith put down her chopsticks, chewed on a crisp sesame cracker, and stared at her sister. "Oh my God," she said a moment later. "You're leaving."

Miranda smiled. "I am." After a pause, she continued.

"It'll be better, right? I mean, you need your space, so do I. You can get another roommate. Or, maybe you don't even need to, you're doing so well at work. I mean, neither of us has had roommates since college and we're both a little past it, right?"

"Okay, confess," Meredith demanded. "Did you fall in love?"

Miranda laughed again. "Yes. With a town."

"What? You're not just moving, you're leaving the city?"

Miranda paused. "I've loved being here with you."

Meredith squinted.

"Most of the time," Miranda amended. "I've loved our house, my Co-op gallery spot, lots of favorite places. It's taught me a lot. And . . . I needed this step, needed to be close to you and within striking distance of our folks."

"Did you miss them that much when you were in Vermont?"

"I think I was too busy as a Bennington student to miss anyone much, except on those l-o-n-g winter nights." Miranda shivered at the memory of fifty-below windchill and howling winds, hardly something any California girl took in stride.

"Bennington was perfect for me," Miranda continued. "The whole mental atmosphere of artistic exploration, personal-best challenges, finding your own voice . . . just what I needed. And we did have work-terms, giving us some real world internships. But being there was also living a sheltered, nurtured life of privilege. So hurling myself into the art world of a major city like SF was daunting.

Being close to Mother and Dad and to you also gave me the certainty that people who cared were near." She looked into her sister's eyes. "You made this huge, intimidating city feel safe, and as comfortable as I can be in a city."

"Oh, Mandy," Meredith said, reaching across the counter to touch her hand.

"And now . . . I'm connecting with my own . . . I don't know if roots is really the right word. But my soul sings by the water and the mountains, where the color is green, and sometimes yellow."

"You painted that, didn't you, before you went on your trip?"

"I did. It felt like a sign."

"So, okay, forgive me for being practical for a moment, but did you get a job? Do you have enough money for the move? Did you find a place to live?"

Miranda took a breath. "I did get a good commission, enough to get me launched."

"Wow."

"And I can stay in someone's guest house for a month while I look for my own place. It's all going to work out," Miranda assured her sister.

Meredith smiled. "Sounds like you're the one who's already *worked* it out." After a pause, she asked, "Told Mother and Dad yet?"

"No. Mother will be concerned, I know. Dad won't mind."

"And that artist's rep you have?"

"Zelda will have a cow."

The two sat in their kitchen laughing until Miranda realized she was also crying.

Miranda put another Metheny cassette in her studio player, then walked into her cheery bedroom. She'd never had time to buy the yellow pillows, she reflected. Maybe she would paint another mural with yellow flowers in her new place.

She'd miss this place. But humming in the background was a kind of joy she'd never known, a sense of freedom and belonging, a boldness that carried her timidity away with a tide of awareness.

The delicate strains of "Letter from Home" drifted through the room, reminding her that ties would never be broken, just expanded. This new road would take her away, but it would also take her toward what she'd need in her life. She already knew Sally, Samantha and Kevin; she had new colleagues with whom she'd shared an artistic adventure. Others would come—more colleagues, friends, maybe someone to love.

She'd stay here through spring. Come summer, all her belongings would be with her in a different place, where breezes would blow off the ocean, up onto the bluffs of the Central Coast. Eucalyptus would perfume the night air, and coastal pines would stand sentinel. Paint would flow from the ends of her brushes as fresh images filled her searching eyes and her wandering soul.

"What do you know? Little Miranda gets a big life," she said aloud.

Then she heard the right reply.

Well, that's what happens when the heart listens.

Cast of Characters

Samantha Hugo: early 50s, 5'9, cognac-brown eyes, redhead, statuesque, sharp dresser; Director of Milford-Haven's Environmental Planning Commission; Miranda's new friend.

Charles Jones: late 50s, 6', green eyes, dark hair with graying temples; father of Meredith and Miranda, married to their mother "Veri" Jones; a fund manager and advisor; elegant member of Bay Area elite society.

Meredith Jones: late 20s, 5'8, teal eyes, medium-length brunet hair, beautiful, shapely, athletic; San Francisco financial advisor; Miranda's elder sister and roommate. Works for a great boss, but wrangles with a sexist colleague; hungry for a romantic relationship.

Miranda Jones: late 20s, 5'9, green eyes, long brunet hair, beautiful, lean, athletic; Meredith's younger sister and roommate; fine artist specializing in watercolors, acrylics and murals; a staunch environmentalist whose paintings often depict endangered species; makes plans to escape her wealthy Bay-Area family to create a new life in Milford-Haven.

Veronica "Veri" Jones: early 50s, 5'7, teal-blue eyes, sleekly coiffed dark mahogany hair, slender but curvy, exceptionally beautiful; mother of Meredith and Miranda; a former dancer. Founder of three non-profits in San Francisco; one of group of founders of Belvedere Community Foundation in 1990; member of Greater Bay Ballet Company.

Ron Mansfield: early 60s, Senior Partner at R&R Investments, old friend to Charles Jones, Meredith's boss, a man she respects and admires, a true mentor.

Zelda McIntyre: early 50s, 5'1, violet eyes, wavy black hair, voluptuous, dramatic and striking; owner of private firm Artist Representations in Santa Barbara; Miranda's artist's rep; corporate art buyer.

Sally O'Mally: early 40s, 5'3, blue eyes, blond curly hair, perfectly proportioned; owner of Sally's Restaurant; owner of Burn-It-Off; born and reared in Arkansas; Miranda's friend; dislikes Samantha; secretly involved with Jack Sawyer.

Kevin Ransom: late 20s, 6'8, hazel eyes, sandy hair, strong jawline, lean, muscular without effort; Foreman at Sawyer Construction; innocent, naive, kind.

Cornelius Smith: early 40s, 6'3, indigo-blue eyes, black hair, handsome, lean; grew up in Milford-Haven where his parents still live.

Peter Sylvester: mid-30s, 6'1, well-built, handsome, black hair; works in the financial industry; met Meredith at a conference; attracted to her and invites her on a day-trip date to the famous French Laundry restaurant; cheats on his wife.

Milford-Haven Recipes
Veri Jones's Easter Brunch
(As prepared by Veri and Pilar at the Jones home)

Goldenrod Eggs

[Serves 4. May be increased to any size]
Ingredients:
>   hard-boiled eggs
> 2 C.   Béchamel Sauce
> 4   toasted English muffins

Preparation:
– Break cooked whites of eggs into pieces and add to Béchamel Sauce.
– Spoon over toasted English muffins.
– Press yolks through fine sieve and sprinkle over top.
– Garnish with paprika and chopped parsley.

Béchamel Sauce

Ingredients:
> 2 T.   butter
> 2 T.   flour
> 1¼ C. milk, heated
> ¼ t.   nutmeg
>   salt & freshly ground white pepper

Preparation:
– Melt butter in saucepan.
– Sprinkle in flour, stirring constantly, until mixture cooks, but do not allow to brown (about 2 minutes).
– Add hot milk, still stirring, as sauce thickens, bringing to boil.
– Lower heat, continue to cook (about 3 more minutes).
– Season with nutmeg, salt & pepper to taste.

Fruit Starter

– begin with cut fruits in season

Meat Platter

– serve with breakfast meats

*Provided by Joan Tassenoy

Milford-Haven Recipes
Thomas Keller's Salmon Cornets
(As enjoyed by Meredith and Peter at The French Laundry)

To find the recipe and preparation instructions,
please purchase *The French Laundry*
by Thomas Keller and Deborah Jones.

or visit one of the following sites:

VanityFair.com
2014
Thomas Keller Salmon Cornet

CarolCookSkeller.Blogspot.com
2008
cornets-salmon-tartare

*Created by Chef Thomas Keller, The French Laundry,
Yountville, CA

Return soon to . . .
Milford-Haven!

Available now . . .

Mara Purl's
When Hummers Dream

the next novelette
in the exciting Milford-Haven saga

Enjoy the following Preview
from the novelette . . .

Chapter 1

Miranda Jones, grasping a mug of warm lemon-tea in one hand, with her other hand slid open the door to her deck, grinning at the complex trill of a robin.

She stepped out into the cool freshness just in time to see the first rays of sun arrow over the ridge behind her house, then race through a thick stand of pines to pierce the Pacific waves dancing in the near distance.

After sinking into a deck chair, she was about to sip her tea when something bulleted past her head. She ducked, nearly spilling her drink. She whipped her head around to discover what it was, but saw no silhouette against the pale sky. *Some kind of flying critter . . . nearly penetrated my ear and flew off with a hank of my hair. Well, not really,* she admitted. *But what was that? Too small to be the robin, too large for a bumble bee. A hummingbird? But why? It's not like I had anything sweet nearby . . . no nectar . . . nothing red.*

Leaving the mystery unsolved, she glanced over at the hammock she'd recently added to her deck furniture.

I've been in Milford-Haven for eight months, but I'm still figuring out what works for my new space, still getting settled. The hammock—a stretched-fabric bed fitted to a metal frame—made her smile. *An indulgence . . . but, it seems perfect right there. That dark green canvas echoes the living room couch . . . blends with the pines out here. . . . I haven't really tried it out, except just for a minute right after Kevin helped me set it up.*

One of several new friends, Kevin Ransom—a tall, quiet guy she'd first met at the hardware store—was employed at a local construction company. He was known around town as someone who knew how to build, assemble, or wire just about anything. Most of all, he was kind. She'd readily accepted his offer to help her install her new hammock, as well as several other items around her new rental house.

I really should try the hammock. A breeze swept across the deck and swirled through the open neck of her fleece. *It's still chilly out. Maybe I should grab my quilt.* She rose and went inside, set her now-cool mug of tea on a living room end table, and grabbed the colorful coverlet draped over the end of the sofa. Returning to the deck, she slid onto the hammock and pulled over her the favorite gift Meredith had special-ordered for her as a moving-away present.

For three and a half years, she and her sister had been roommates in San Francisco: Mer, the successful financial adviser; Mandy the struggling artist. Things had started to change when her manager Zelda "discovered" her, and her paintings began to sell in some of the city's best galleries.

Recently, Mer had delivered photos of some of Miranda's landscape paintings to a local craftswoman who offered a unique service: she'd reproduce photographic images onto soft cotton squares, then sew them into quilts. The paintings Meredith had chosen now traced across the fabric like windows into their childhoods: the blues of beach-days; the greens of forest walks; the lavenders of north-coast sunsets. *So thoughtful of Mer. I love it!*

Snuggling under the puffy quilt, Miranda sank comfortably back against the pillows to savor the gentle movement of the hammock while her gaze traced the sunrays that bypassed her deck to shatter into diamonds on the surface of the waves.

Love catching these first moments of the day. Gives me a head start. Though her logic-mind might still be half-asleep, her artist-eyes were already at work. *The colors . . . they're never the same. This morning the clouds scudding by are lemon-custard; the sea is teal, where I can see it. And the pines seem soft, as though carved of candle wax.*

But even as she tried to continue cataloguing the details that her painter's eyes couldn't help but notice, her lids began to close as the gentle motion of the hammock lulled her into a early-morning nap.

Miranda heard a faint hissing sound and began walking toward it. Sprinklers, *she thought,* I must be near a garden.

A high hedge climbed in the morning mist and parted in the middle where she moved through, her bare legs tingling from the low, gentle spray of water that misted through the plantings.

In the drenched garden, ferns arced up to her shoulders; thick ivy draped down over a high fence; raised beds dripped with bleeding hearts; and curving pathways swirled with rainbow arrays of impatiens.

I don't see them, but I smell roses. *At a far corner, she glimpsed a charming arched trellis and went toward it for a closer look. She reached out to touch the inch-thick stem of the sturdy plants twined through its lattice, but jerked back her hand when a huge thorn pierced her finger.* Why would there be a thorn? Unless . . . this stem is twenty feet high and two inches thick . . . but it's a rose bush!

A single drop of blood oozed from her fingertip, to fall in slow motion onto the fertile ground. As Miranda continued to watch that spot, a tiny green shoot pushed its way through the soil, climbing steadily upward till it reached her shoulder. Then a bud appeared and opened into a single red rose.

As she leaned to inhale its rich fragrance, a hummingbird raced her for the privilege, pushing his long bill deep into the heart of the flower.

Then the hummer turned to face her, winked, and zoomed past her ear.

Miranda blinked her eyes open with a start. *Was someone just watching me?* She glanced around her deck. *No, of course not. Yet I feel a presence of some kind. Of course I know the local critters are always watching. . . .*

Peeling back the quilt, she threw her legs over the side of the hammock, stood, and stretched. *Wonder how long I napped?* She looked toward the east, noticing the sun now rode higher above the mountains. *Probably an hour or so. Time to get moving.*

She thought of her plan for the day: to paint the flora and fauna at a favorite spot, the Rosencrantz Café and Guildenstern Garden. The whimsical name—which always made her smile— hinted at the style of the place: part history, part culture, part nature. A lovely redwood-and-glass structure set atop a hill, it overlooked the ocean and was angled to take advantage of the view north toward the Santa Carlita Cove and the Piedras Blancas Lighthouse beyond.

The spacious back yard of the café offered a series of redwood decks surrounded by a garden and its adjoining nursery. The owners, Robin and George—who'd used their *R* and *G* to improvise the name—were committed to featuring Central Coast varietals, and were well versed in the history and genus of each plant they carried.

The profusion of indigenous and imported species,

the myriad colors and the charming architecture of the garden's paths, fountains and seating areas not only had made the R&G a revelation to tourists who happened by, but also had created a loyal following among local residents.

For a wildlife and landscape artist like Miranda, it provided a research library and laboratory. Recently, she'd made arrangements with Lucy, the restaurant manager, to spend six hours in the garden. She'd tried for a day mid-week, but for liability reasons, Robin had suggested the Friday-through-Sunday schedule, when they had more staff, would be best. Meanwhile Miranda'd already visited several times, filling pages of her artist-journal with sketches and watercolor studies. *Now I'm ready for a day of painting fully completed pieces.*

She'd need her folding art-table—the one she used in place of an easel when she painted with watercolor—to hold her work level and allow her to control the movement of her liquid colors. *And I'll need a hat, brush carrier, small water bottles. . . .*

Grabbing the quilt from the hammock, she went inside, draped the coverlet back over the sofa, and walked into her adjacent studio to gather the day's materials.

A few minutes later, with her supplies packed and waiting by her front door, she ran downstairs to shower and dress.

Lucy Seecor tossed her long, black braid over one shoulder and began to count out the flatware. The bright blue napkins were already laid out, ready to wrap the silver.

"Expecting any larger groups today, Luce?"

Lucy glanced up and watched for a moment as her boss unloaded a carrier tray of glasses. "Just the Ragged Point Book Club ladies. It's their monthly meeting."

"Right. They're a nice group. What time are they booked?"

"Not till one o'clock," Lucy replied, not missing a beat in her work with the silver.

Robin shook his head. "Never can figure out how you keep the whole month's schedule in your brain. Not that I'm complaining!"

Lucy chuckled.

"Anything else going on today?"

"Just Miranda Jones."

"Oh! That's today! I'd forgotten. Anything I need to prepare?"

"Already got it handled," Lucy said.

"Of course you do!" Robin shook his head again. "As always. Okay, then, I'll be in the kitchen."

As Robin left to resume his culinary duties, Lucy paused for a moment, looking out the huge picture window at the spectacular ocean view, so adored by the restaurant patrons.

Miranda Jones . . . so dedicated to her art. Hope I can grab a moment to see how she does it. Always wanted to paint. Never had the time. Well, maybe one day. . . .

Miranda rolled her vintage Mustang to a stop in the grav-
eled parking lot of the R&G Café & Garden. *R&G . . . that's
what the regulars call it. Looks like I'm getting here early
enough . . . no other cars parked yet.*

She grabbed her watercolor bag and folded table,
then entered via the nursery—walking through display aisles of potted plants and small, burbling fountains—until she emerged at the entrance to the garden
itself.

Out in the open again, she glanced up at the sky to
check the light. *Slight haze . . . nice. It'll act like a giant
diffuser.* She looked around at the redwood tables, raised
flower beds, winding pathways, and lamp posts with
hanging baskets, as she considered the best location for
her day's work.

As her gaze rotated across the open space, she
paused, captured by an unexpected perfection. Across
the garden, a glass wall acted as a windbreak for guests
who chose to eat outside. The uprights supporting the
glass perfectly framed a view of the ocean. *Well . . . there
it is . . . a ready-made painting if I ever saw one.*

She moved forward, watching closely as the visual
frame adjusted, then she backed up again, choosing the
ideal position. Grinning at the serendipity of the find, she
placed her bag on the ground and set up her worktable.
Before I set up my supplies, I should look for Lucy.

Miranda went the rest of the way across the garden
and opened one of the double glass doors that led inside. On the ground level, a long, polished bar ran along a

mirrored wall and small round tables spread across the floor—all deserted till evening. She took the stairs up to the restaurant, pausing as she reached the top to gaze out at the view, even more stunning from this higher level.

"Hi, Miranda." The restaurant manager Lucy approached with a smile, hand outstretched. "Welcome! We've been expecting you."

"Good to see you again, Lucy. I'm really looking forward to this. Can I show you where I was thinking of setting up?"

"Sure." Lucy led the way downstairs and onto the terraced exterior, glimpsing Miranda's table and bag. "Oh, that should be fine."

"I won't be in the way of any of your customers?"

"No. Actually, I think they'll be intrigued." Lucy chuckled. "Who knows, you might become a new tourist attraction!"

"Oh, I hope not!" Miranda tried to hide a grimace. "I'll do my best to be inconspicuous."

"Uh . . . would you mind if. . . ."

"What?" Miranda encouraged.

"Well, I'd love to watch you paint. I mean, I doubt I'll have much time, but if I can sneak away . . . would it bother you?"

"No! Not at all."

"Really? Oh, that's great! So, can I bring you anything? A glass of raspberry iced tea?"

Miranda couldn't help but smile at the childlike exuberance, then said, "I'll save that special treat to have with lunch. Well, I think I'll get started before your customers start to arrive."

"Enjoy!" Lucy tossed her long braid over her shoulder, and returned to her duties inside.

Miranda reached down to open her bag. As she pulled out her portable watercolor palette with its small individual pans, her mind automatically cataloged how she'd mix the gradations of color from the few primary shades she kept in her travel kit. She'd squeeze color from the tubes—warm colors on the right, cool on the left.

A loud buzzing whizzed by her ear and she glanced up in time to see a hummingbird speed across the garden at eye level. *So it probably was a hummer that buzzed me this morning! Perfect. He'll be part of my painting today. That's a rufous . . . jewel-bright and aggressive.*

Of the 356 species of hummingbird she'd read about and watched on film in recent years, she knew the rufous migration patterns meant this was their time of year to be on California's Central Coast. In October, the tiny birds winged all the way back to Mexico for the winter.

The iridescence of the species posed a special challenge to making the jewel-tone feathers look realistic, but she knew how to handle it. She always packed her Daniel Smith Luminescent, a special additive that could be mixed into any color, making it appear pearlescent.

Okay, now water and brushes. She rummaged in her bag, pulling out her favorite small water bottle that, when squeezed, pushed out a supply of clean water into a small well on its top. She brought out her selection of brushes: three round—sizes two, four and six—and two flat—sizes two and four.

Next she reviewed the media she'd brought. First were her trusty three-by-five and five-by-seven watercolor blocks—heavy pads of paper from which sheets could later be removed individually. Second were a few differently sized Ampersand Claybords-for-watermedia —masonite wood panels with their special water-and-paper layers added to one side, ideal for creating small, collectible pieces. *I think I'll start with the smallest Claybords, experiment a bit and get the colors right.* These'd have to be sealed, later, with clear acrylic spray so the images wouldn't wash off. That reminded her she'd need her tiny spray water bottle to keep the paint liquid in case it started to dry too fast.

With her portable studio ready, Miranda pulled two more things from her bag—a wide-brimmed folding straw hat, which she popped right onto her head; and one of her three-by-three Claybords. Now she stood quietly, inhaled, then bent her knees and began shifting her weight in a *Tai Chi* brush-knee movement. After a few rotations, she picked up her palette, her number two flat brush, and began to paint.

Return soon to ...
Milford-Haven!

Available now ...

Mara Purl's
What the Heart Knows

the first novel
in the exciting Milford-Haven saga

Enjoy the following Preview
from the novel . . .

Chapter 1

The autumn storm tore at the clouds covering Milford-Haven, revealing a swollen moon that hung over a coastline frothy with agitated surf.

Miranda Jones watched the distant flash of the lighthouse for a moment, then looked away from her window to focus on a narrow band of thick paper scrolled across her studio floor. Inhaling deeply, she dipped the tapered fibers of her immense paintbrush and struggled to lift its wet mass from the inky bucket, then swept a black streak across the white paper.

She held the three-inch diameter brush handle upright—its top reaching to her waist—and resumed her bent-knee, wide-footed stance. Hoisting the fully saturated brush, she began the dance that would drag it rhythmically along the paper, creating a vertical image.

Placing her bare feet on the sheet, she stepped backwards, the weight of the sodden brush causing her arms to shake. Yet each motion synchronized with both the soft *shakuhachi* flute music that played over her stereo, and with the call the paper itself seemed to be whispering in her ear.

When she reached the end of the sheet, she walked back to her starting point, replaced the brush in its bucket, and stood entranced, her soul soaking up the experience even as the image soaked into the paper.

By now her studio was permeated with the distinct aroma of the *sumi* ink. Concocted of palm ash and glue, it also contained traces of camphor and musk oil. She inhaled again, agreeing with the legend that promised the ink's special odor helped to induce the perfect meditative state.

She'd placed four black stones—smoothed and rounded from tumbling for years through the nearby surf—as weights to hold the scroll in place. Now they almost blended into the image, as though she'd added four extra smudges of ink. But, in fact, the stones would be removed and weren't part of what she'd painted. She scrutinized the piece. *When the stones are removed, will the piece look incomplete? Yes . . . it needs something more.*

She *felt* the idea, more than she *thought* it. Focusing on an unfilled portion of the paper, she reached for a smaller brush that stood ready in its own bucket. She lifted it, then let her hand sweep through a series of motions. When she'd replaced the smaller brush, she closed her eyes and bowed over the paper, signaling the completion of the current scroll. *My teacher would add a touch of vermillion . . . but I'm not ready for that yet.*

During art school a few years earlier, she'd completed a course on *sumi-e*, and since then she'd occasionally used the ancient Japanese ink-wash painting as both a meditation and a discipline. Traditionally, it was both, from the almost ritualistic grinding of the ink stone into water, to the careful handling of brushes whose hairs were trimmed to a delicate point.

But more recently she'd been accepted into a workshop by the eminent American calligrapher Barbara Bash, who'd shared her unique approach of pouring *sumi* ink from half-gallon bottles and using an oversized brush to create her huge scrolls. *I'll never master this the way Barbara has, but I love how it centers my mind. It's all about flow.*

Is this a "head" or a "heart" process? If "head" was the answer, it wouldn't be in an intellectual sense, because the ink almost seemed to be "thought-projected" onto the paper, the marks capturing a flow of movement uninterrupted by editorializing.

Though the actual painting of the ink-wash was necessarily quick, preparing for each piece was a lengthier process. *At least it is for a relatively inexperienced calligrapher like me.* The ink had to be poured, the paper laid, and the artist had to summon both energy and vision.

Miranda appreciated that this big-brush technique worked on three levels. As physical exercise, it felt similar to Tai Chi and to Yoga, both of which she enjoyed. As mental discipline, its immediacy permitted no distraction, no procrastination. A brush pressed a moment too long would cause ink to soak through and ruin both the paper and the image. She carried these lessons into her own watercolor work.

And though technically big-brush *sumi-e* was certainly a form of fine art, it was far enough away from her core practices of watercolor and acrylics, that it left her free from internal judgment. She could float above the brush, the paper and the image, allowing thoughts and feelings to surface freely. *I know why I love it so much. It lets my heart speak.*

The CD she was listening to came to an end, and a gust of wind rattled the windows. *How many images have I done tonight? The new one makes four. And how long have I been at this? I've lost track of time again.* She glanced out at the moon, noting it was lower now, its color beginning to shift from silver to gold as it sank toward the ocean. *It'll set soon, and we'll have some black sky before dawn, so I'll have a chance to sleep a little. I think I'm finished work for tonight.*

Stepping to her worktable, she picked up her X-acto knife and carefully sliced below the end of the painted image, separating it from the heavy roll. She lifted the top edge enough to drag the long sheet parallel to the others, which were laid out on the studio floor to dry. Tomorrow she'd mount the stepladder and tack the vertical images to the wall. For now, she stared down at the new work and its three companion pieces, finished earlier that evening.

She stood back to examine the four scrolls. "Oh!" she exclaimed. "It's the four seasons!" Amazed this hadn't occurred to her before, she now saw clearly that the four six-foot-high water paintings described the subtle elements of California's coastal seasons: a pine for winter; a blooming crape myrtle for spring; an olive tree for summer; and a persimmon for autumn. *Maybe I didn't notice at first because the images are black-and-white.*

The piece she'd just finished was of the persimmon tree, its drooping leaves and multi-stemmed trunk so reminiscent of Asia. Yet she learned they'd been imported to California in the 1800s, and they were now as much a part of the Central Coast as any native tree. The bright orange color of the fruit came into her mind, highlighting the fall season when it ripened.

She glanced down at the bottom corner, where she'd added that final swirl of paint. *What is it? It looks like . . . a kitten!* Kneeling, she inspected the small image more carefully. *I know I had no particular definition in mind when I created it.* She remembered laying the wet brush sideways, then dotting it here and there as she lifted it off the page. But now, there they were, the distinct feline features—head and whiskers, tail and feet.

"Hello," she said to the impish picture. "Thanks for the visit!"

Tired to the bone, Miranda stood, stretched and sighed. *Now for the cleanup.* It took her a good half hour to wash the brushes, empty the buckets, and secure anything else she might've left open in her workspace. By the time she flipped the light switch and headed downstairs to her bedroom, she was already half asleep.

I'll shower in the morning, she thought. *But it's already morning!* Too tired to make sense of the chronology, she washed her face, brushed her teeth and collapsed under her comforter. *It'd be nice to cuddle up with that little kitty I drew.* She smiled at the fantasy and imagined the kitty tiptoeing across the covers.

Those four scrolls . . . they're great, but I'd love to do them in full color. Maybe I can take the four seasons idea and incorporate it into my miniature watercolor post-cards. . . .

As she reached to turn out the light on her nightstand, something caused her to choke. Gasping, she reached for the water bottle she kept handy by the bed, sputtering as she took a gulp. *What in the world?* It wasn't as though she'd gagged on a morsel of food, or swallowed down the wrong pipe. She'd been choking *before* she took the swig of water.

She shuddered, trying to sense the source of whatever she might be feeling. *Is something bad about to happen?*

No, not in Milford-Haven, she reassured herself. *Bad things don't happen here.*

Jack Sawyer's alarm clock stuttered into life, its plastic frame cracked from abuse. A heavy hand swept down and banged the "snooze" button, then retreated under the covers.

Jack hadn't slept well. Keeping one step ahead of

town, county, and state regulations didn't usually keep him up at night. But now he had to contend with Samantha. No matter what he did, he could never seem to get away from that woman.

He swung his legs out from under the blanket and didn't notice its long-forgotten coffee stains. He focused for a moment on the clock's digital display. The last digit no longer illuminated, so it was always a guess. He hoped it was still within a minute or two of 7 a.m.

Jack headed down the hall, his bare feet leaving an occasional imprint in the dusty floor. An hour-and-a-half from now, he'd be in his office and the irritating phone calls would start: from contractors trying to pick his brains; from prospects who said other contractors could outbid him; from incompetent workers with idiotic questions; from inspectors with nasty notices. But at least his *home* phone wouldn't ring, and he wouldn't turn on his cell till later. Plus—today held the promise of a new client.

He reached the bathroom and scowled at himself in the mirror. The fierce blue eyes were still clear. The hair had gone salt-and-pepper, the face a little jowly. Chest and arms remained firm, thanks to the fact he spent about as much time on his job sites as behind his desk. Jack's gaze trailed down the rest of his six-foot frame— solidly packed with muscle, but with a little too much gut. *Not bad for over fifty. Besides, only one thing really matters. Everything still functions.*

Just then, his home phone did begin to ring. *Damn!*

Who the hell would be calling me now? A sudden fit of coughing seized him, loud enough that he missed the next two rings of his phone, and on the fourth one his answering machine picked up.

"This is Jack Sawyer. I'm out. Leave a message if you expect me to call you back." He paid no attention to his own gravelly voice on the outgoing message. But after the beep, when an authoritative female voice began speaking, Jack started coughing again.

"Jack, this is Sam calling." As if he didn't know. *"I'll leave a message at your office, but in case you don't go there this morning, you should know you'll be facing an injunction. Have a nice day."*

Kevin Ransom loved the mornings better than any other time of day. In autumn, it was still dark and chilly when he got up. He never knew whether the sky would look pink or orange or lavender, so it was always a surprise. He liked that best of all.

The view from Kevin's porch raced down a steep incline through a stand of tall California pines. The smallness of the house was made up for by the size of the trees, which stood on protected land, so they'd never be cut down. The first rays of light penetrated the upper branches like the strobe lights of a *National Geographic* photographer. *Guess the storm last night cleared out all the clouds.*

The squirrel who occupied the back yard stepped

onto the railing of the deck and walked gingerly toward Kevin, chattering for his morning nut. Today it would be a cashew, and Kevin couldn't decide whether his squirrel was demanding an early Halloween treat, or stocking up for winter.

Kevin only had a few minutes before he had to leave for work. He liked to get there before Mr. Sawyer and make sure the coffee was made. It sometimes seemed to make Mr. Sawyer's mood a little better.

"Hey, little fella." He spoke quietly so as not to scare the squirrel off. "Want another one?" he asked. He wondered why it was always so much easier to talk to animals than it was to talk to people.

Sally O'Mally unlocked the back door of her restaurant and flipped on the kitchen lights, illuminating the gleaming steel sinks, pristine countertops, and the rows of shiny pans that hung from a large overhead rack. She caught the room's faint odor of fresh lemons that lingered after last night's cleaning. Though she'd been tired when she woke up this morning, she felt a spark of energy at seeing her workspace spotless and ready for a new day.

Mama trained me well. Still, I never do get up as early as she does. She pictured her mother in Arkansas, still living on the farm, still knitting, and still baking up a storm—biscuits, breads, and her signature pies.

Gotta get the first pot o' coffee started. After putting her shoulder bag in the tiny private office she'd created out of a closet, she pulled the plastic lid off an industrial-sized tin of ground coffee, loaded several scoops into a filter paper, then snapped the basket-holder into place. *Okay, now for the biscuits. Maybe I can get the first batch in before June gets here.*

Her hands moved almost by their own volition as they found the chilled batter—prepared the night before—in the fridge, greased the baking sheets, dusted the cutting board, rolled out the dough and began pressing into it a round cutter. When the sheets were ready for the oven, she slid them in. Just then the back door swung open again.

"Mornin', Sal," June called cheerily in her distinctive Brooklyn accent. "Geez, it's gettin' light a lot later already!"

"Well, that's September for ya," Sally confirmed. "How you doin' this mornin'?"

"Fine."

Sally smiled at the long sound of June's vowels. *I s'ppose I sound just as funny to her as she does to me. Milford-Haven brings in all kinds.*

Sawyer Construction Company was still closed and locked when early-morning sunlight slid past decade-old layers of dust on the Venetian blinds. There was no sign of life until the light on the office answering machine illuminated, and the cassette tape began to squeal softly while it turned.

Jack's outgoing message crackled over the speaker. The voice did nothing to belie the gruff impatience that set the tone at his office. *"You've reached Sawyer Construction. We're out of the office at the moment, but leave your name, number and a brief message, and we'll get back to you shortly. Wait for the beep."*

"Jack, it's Samantha. I read in the paper this morning that you've announced the start of construction on that shopping center." Not even the filtering of the tiny speaker on his machine could make her voice small. *"You know perfectly well the plans have not yet been approved by the Planning Commission. I'd advise you to call me the minute you get to your office."*

COLOPHON

The print version of this book is set in the Cambria font, released in 2004 by Microsoft, as a formal, solid font to be equally readable in print and on screens. It was designed by Jelle Bosma, Steve Matteson, and Robin Nicholas.

The name Cambria is the classical name for Wales, the Latin form of the Welsh name for Wales, *Cymru*. The etymology of *Cymru* is *combrog*, meaning "compatriot."

The California town of Cambria is named for its resemblance to the south-western coast of Wales, where the town of Milford Haven has existed since before ancient Roman times, and is mentioned in William Shakespeare's *Cymbeline.*

The dingbat is the *Sinum cymba*, drawn by artist Mary Helsaple. The common name is the concave ear moon snail shell, inhabited by a marine gastropod mollusk in the *Naticidae* family. The spiral formation resembles the cochlea, or inner ear, which is shaped like a snail shell in order to boost sensitivity to low frequencies.

LIGHTHOUSE

Each of the Milford-Haven Novellas features a real lighthouse. In the case of this prequel in the Milford-Haven saga, the featured lighthouse is part history, part imagination.

The real lighthouse, pictured, is part of the historic Chapman Estate in Shell Beach, California. The oceanside property holds an English Tudor-style mansion, built in 1930, and a windmill, added in 1934, which pumps sea water into the estate's pool. The lighthouse was built in 1948 by then-owner Arthur Rogers to provide privacy. Clifford Chapman purchased the estate in 1962. Chapman and his partner Don Seidler added a koi pond, pavilion, and solarium, and turned the estate into a hub for artists, musicians, and writers.

Chapman and Seidler also opened their estate to local non-profit organizations for fund-raising events as well as neighborhood and family celebrations. In keeping with their spirit of inclusion and generosity, Clifford Chapman established a trust and gifted the estate to the City of Pismo Beach, which accepted the gift in 2013. The estate offers tours and is rented for special events. For more information please visit www.ChapmanEstateFoundation.org.

The fictional lighthouse included in this novella is loosely based upon the Chapman Estate's, but is located in Milford-Haven with a history of its own, as described in this story, and further developed in later books in the series.

Secret of the Shells

*Special Messages about a Woman and Her Self,
and about Discovering the Next Chapter . . . of Her Life*

 Ear Moon Shell: When the Heart Listens

▸ This shell belongs to a marine gastropod, with its spiral shell a match to the human cochlea, or inner ear, designed to capture low frequencies. It refers to the quality of listening both externally and internally in this book.

▸ How important do you consider listening to be? Are you a good listener? Do you think good listening can improve a situation? Can internal listening offer guidance?

▸ What would you do if your intuition told you to move to a new location that you didn't know much about, but felt would work for you?

▸ What does "listening to the heart" actually mean? Do you feel people can sometimes hear voices? Or do you think the "heart" communicates through feelings?

▸ Have you ever gone on a trip and "fallen in love" with the location you visited? Write down the qualities of that special place. Can you find those qualities where you live now? Or would you have to move to find them?

▸ How important is money when you're making plans? Is it important to have a sizable amount set aside before putting plans in place? Or do the plans come first, trusting that necessary funds will follow?

▸ Create a hypothetical plan for something you have always wanted to do. Include all the details you can think of including funds, logistics, support system, training, colleagues, and so forth. Use this as a Vision Document and track what happens once you have created it.

To discover more about the Secrets of the Shells
visit www.MaraPurl.com.

To reach the author, by e-mail: MaraPurl@MaraPurl.com.
by mail: Mara Purl c/o Milford-Haven Enterprises
PO Box 7304-629
North Hollywood, CA 91603

When the Heart Listens

Reading Group Topics for Discussion

1. The novellas and novelettes in this series stand alone, while the novels are written in more of a serial format. Do you prefer stories that have a traditional beginning, middle and end? Or do you prefer a serial story?

2. The main location for the series of novels is Milford-Haven. However, this is a prequel, occurring before the protagonist discovers the town and then decides to move there. Is it interesting or helpful to read this "background" story?

3. The story focuses on protagonist Miranda Jones, who currently lives in the world of art in San Francisco. How would you describe her feelings about her sometimes competitive career in the big city? Is she irresponsible about money? Should income be the focus of a career?

4. This novella also focuses on Miranda's relationship with her sister Meredith. What is your impression of Meredith? Do you admire her business sense and financial success? Why does she disapprove of her artsy sister? Do they make good roommates?

5. This book shows a lot of interaction between Miranda, Meredith, and their parents. Do their parents strike the right balance of being supportive about their daughters, or do they meddle?

6. A protagonist should have some solid, recurring qualities, but also should grow and learn from her experiences. Does Miranda grow and learn? Does she overthink her decisions? Does she truly follow her intuition in deciding to move?

7. Were you surprised by Meredith's romantic behavior? Do you feel she should have known better than to date the man she did? Or do you think she was genuinely hoodwinked, and did a good job coming clean about a tricky situation?

8. In addition to being a writer, Mara Purl is also an actress who has performed in theatre and on television, as well as co-writing the book *Act Right*. Do you feel her understanding of characters and their behavior makes her writing more realistic?

9. Why is this book called *When the Heart Listens*? Do you believe Miranda, or any other characters, actually listened to their "heart" or intuitive information? Do you feel this gave them legitimate guidance?

To share or print these discussion points please visit:
http://marapurl.com/books/when-the-heart-listens

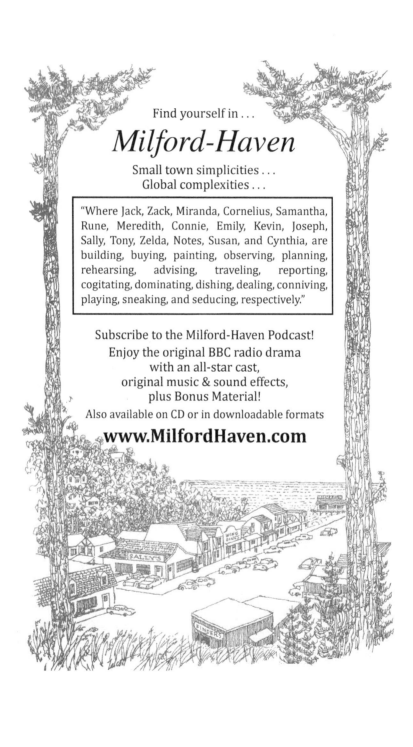

Mara Purl, author of the popular and critically acclaimed *Milford-Haven Novels*, pioneered small-town fiction for women.

Mara's beloved fictitious town has been delighting audiences since 1992, when it first appeared as *Milford-Haven, U.S.A.©*—the first American radio drama ever licensed and broadcast by the BBC. The show reached an audience of 4.5 million listeners in the U.K. In the U.S., it was the 1994 Finalist for the New York Festivals World's Best Radio Programs.

Mara was named the Top Female Author for Fiction by *The Authors Show*, and to date, her books have won more than thirty-five book awards including the American Fiction, Benjamin Franklin, National Indie Excellence, USA Book News Best Books, and ForeWord Books of the Year.

Mara's other writing credits include plays, screenplays, scripts for *Guiding Light*, cover stories for *Rolling Stone*, staff writing at the *Financial Times (of London)*, and the Associated Press. She is the co-author (with Erin Gray) of *Act Right: A Manual for the On-Camera Actor*.

As an actress, Mara was "Darla Cook" on *Days of Our Lives*. For the one-woman show *Mary Shelley: In Her Own Words*—which Mara performs and co-wrote (with Sydney Swire)—she earned a Peak Award; she has co-starred in multiple productions of *Sea Marks* by Gardner McKay, and plays the title role in *Becoming Julia Morgan*. She was named one of twelve Women of the Year by the Los Angeles County Commission for Women.

Mara is married to Dr. Larry Norfleet and lives in Los Angeles, and in Colorado Springs.

Visit her website at www.MaraPurl.com where you can subscribe to her newsletter and link to her social media sites. She welcomes e-mail from readers at MaraPurl@MaraPurl.com.

CPSIA information can be obtained
at www.ICGtesting.com
Printed in the USA
LVHW042134191020
669177LV00004BA/1030